Fiction Foremost

A Compiled Collection of Short Stories

Parker James

Cover Design by うさぎMaylen
ISBN: 9798894438955

DEDICATION

This dedication goes out to the same people of my first novel and to those who continue to support me. Thank you all for helping me achieve my dreams.

CONTENT WARNING

Some of these stories deal with mature scenarios and themes. Some are inspired by cultures and mythologies from around the world. To maintain authenticity, I used proper terms and names where I could, but included a brief explanation and pronunciation for ones not widely known in the footnotes. Thank you for reading and I hope you enjoy.

CONTENTS

1 Pyrrhic Victory   1

2 Late Game   12

3 Perpetual Pictures   22

4 Harry Hawthorn V. His Characters,   31

5 A Star of Ash: A Tale from Saigōhon   41

6 A Star of Ash: Their First Souls of Saints Day   57

What's Coming Next   64

Follow the Author   65

PYRRHIC VICTORY

Pilot Assistance Program Online... Last Mission Log? = 07/03/2105 Operation Bastion... Status? = Failure... Mission Brief? = The U.X.C. were discovered by multiple national space programs (De-Classified as Unidentified Xeno Combatant.) Through the coordination of the United Nations Office for Outer Space Affairs, the investigation concluded that the U.X.C had hostile intentions as they had eradicated every planet on their way to Earth. They were classified as the next extinction level event...

Survival was prioritized. Every nation under the U.N. had conscripted all eligible candidates for military duty. The N.O.F. (Near Orbit Fleet) would serve as the first line of defense and M.A.I.C. (Mechanized Assault Infantry Corp) the last. As the invasion date drew closer, candidacy eligibility requirements were broadened to conscript more recruits. If N.O.F casualties exceed 50%, standing orders are for all evacuation vessels to launch and remain in hiding until an all-clear signal is given...

On 07/01/2105, the U.X.C. invaded. In less than 72 hours, the U.X.C. forces overwhelmed the N.O.F. The evacuation order was sent. The M.A.I.C. was deployed and subsequently eradicated. All other Earth defenses had been eliminated with little resistance...

Casualty Status? = N.O.F. Deployed 300,000 ships of various classes, from military to civilian evacuation vessels. 12 are M.I.A, and the rest are confirmed K.I.A. Civilian population was last recorded pre-Operation Bastion as 9 billion. Current reports and life sign detections indicate... Calculating... <10,000 remain and rapidly reducing... M.A.I.C casualties? = <7,000,000 units were deployed. Scans indicate... Calculating... 5 pilot life signs remain scattered across the continents... 2 Mechanized combat suits remain operational...

***

"Nuclear core power reroute complete. Life support at 50%. Radiation Shielding at 15%. Weapons at 10%. User interfaces at 5%. Beginning Pilot self diagnostic scan ... Scan complete. Pilot C-1-52 has suffered numerous injuries; currently unconscious but stable. Attempting to revive Pilot..."

I shrieked out a curse when I was forced back into consciousness and banged my head on the cockpit ceiling. The administered revival drugs had a nasty kick to them; specially when you aren't expecting them. I could hear my heart pounding like an engine piston, and I was just as sweaty as one. I'm ninety percent certain this drug isn't safe. I doubt M.A.I.C. gave a shit about what happened to us since we couldn't even consent to the infusion pump surgery. 'Survival is victory! One life for ten!' and all the other bullcrap.

"Pilot C-1-52, please confirm current status," P.A.P. ordered.

I tried to respond, but I was so disoriented, "Wait? What happened? We were fighting off the-"

"Pilot C-1-52, please confirm current status, or we will inject an additional 200 mgs of revival medication."

"No! No! This is Pilot C-1-52 Chauffy Trebrek reporting! Minor injuries, but nothing too serious." I rattled off before that monotonous A.I. accidentally overdosed me. I didn't hear any more gunfire, explosions, or my geiger ticking from U.X.C.'s Null Matter bombs. Perhaps the battle was finally over?

"Affirmative. Reinstating pilot C-1-52 to active duty."

I ignored it as I looked through the hundreds of lights, buttons, and switches, trying to find the radio. We conscripts were barely taught how to use these suits beyond the essentials of pushing this stick to move, pulling that trigger to shoot, and pressing the button to sacrifice yourself for humanity. I managed to find the radio through all the mess, and I hoped someone else on the other end knew how to use one.

"Hey I'm on the 52nd Auxiliary channel. Pilot Conscript Rank 1. I'm not dead." But there was only static, "I repeat, this is Pilot C-1-52. I am active again. Do you hear me?" Again, there was no response. Piece of crap low-bidder tech.

"Have the comms been damaged?" I asked, not seeing anything obviously broken with it.

"Negative. No communications have been reported in the last 16 hours." P.A.P. answered after performing a diagnostic.

That wasn't right. Why was no one on comms for that long? If the battle was over the all-clear signal should have been going off.

"No, no, no, no, no. S-Something else must be going on!" I said as I flipped through other Auxiliary, even Legion channels, and still nothing. I would have tried the N.O.F. channels, but those were classified to us conscripts.

"Any jamming?" I hoped.

"Negative."

"Electro pulses?" I begged.

"Negative."

"Alright… Alright… Remain calm… Remain… Goddammit!" Even if the drugs weren't making me feel like I had drank ten shots of pure caffeine, if what I had thought was true, no one could have remained calm.

"Turn on the view screens!" I croaked out after kicking one of the panels.

"Full visuals engaged." P.A.P. said before my control board lit up with a full view of my surroundings.

We had lost...

I was deployed near one of the evacuation shelters in New Canonto City. It was a loud, cramped, bustling city. It was full of green plants intertwined with a rainbow of neon lights. I would have dreamed of living there if I could have afforded it. Now, I'll never get the chance. A blanket of black snow seemed to cover every surface, absorbing what little light was left and swallowing all depth and detail. All of the tall buildings had collapsed into ruins. The very ground was scorched into a dark glass. The sky... Oh, God, the sky! It was gone... It was gone, not like nighttime. There were no clouds, no moon, no stars, no sun. Just an ever-consuming void. I felt like I was being sucked in just staring at it. My stomach churned, but there was nothing to vomit.

"Warning, heart-rate elevating to dangerous levels!" P.A.P. tried to warn.

I pushed the throttle and joystick away as I screamed, "I have to get out. P.A.P Open the hatch now!"

"Negative. U.X.C. has released toxins into the atmosphere. Unprotected exposure has been reported to cause cancero-"

My fist bruised as it wailed on the cockpit, "I don't give a damn! Just open the hatch! Let me out of here!"

"Override engaged. Be sure to wear the environmental mask before the airlocks disengage."

I yanked the mask out of the compartment as the air seals puffed out and released the hatch. I pulled myself out and rolled onto the hard glass ground. It knocked the wind out of me, and all I could do was focus on breathing through the thick mask, staring at the void where the sky used to be. There was no sound beyond my heart racing and my own filtered gasps. I didn't think I would have wanted the ear-splitting sounds of battle to return so badly.

***

I could not tell if I blacked out or not. There was no difference whether I closed my eyes or looked at the sky. I needed sound, any sound. I felt like I was going insane If I wasn't sure I already had.

"P.A.P.?" I croaked, "P.A.P. Please?" There was something surreal, pleading with a thirty-ton walking tank. It was essentially a small metal dome with four thick legs with treads on the shins, one arm carrying a massive rail gun, and another was just a bed of missiles mostly spent.

"Zrrt Affirmative. How may I assist you, Pilot C-1-52?" P.A.P. responded through the P.A. system.

"I... I don't know."

"How may I assist you, Pilot C-1-52?" It repeated.

"Can you... tell me, what happened? How did I get knocked out?" **"Are you attempting to request a report of events leading up to your unconscious state 16 hours from this moment?"**

"16 hours?" I sat up, my back aching, "Why did you wait so long to wake me?"

"Nuclear Core was damaged. Needed to prioritize venting and rerouting power."

"Oh, crap!" I jumped up ready to run like hell, "Are you going to meltdown?"

The last thing I needed was to be sitting right next to a mini-Chernobyl.

"Negative, the core has been contained. Radiation shielding was engaged to prevent harmful leakage on the Pilot."

Well, at least it had passed one safety inspection. I used to work on these things in the factory before I was drafted and they were most certainly a rush job.

"So what happened?" I asked.

"After N.O.F. was eradicated , all M.A.I.C. forces were deployed." "Mother fu- Yes, I know that part. Skip ahead."

"After 56 hours of continuous fighting, a U.X.C. vessel began a collision course toward pilot C-2-52. Based on the trajectory, it is likely that this was intentional. Based on your vital records, in an exhausted delirium, you used this suit to try and shield your subordinate. The impact rendered you unconscious."

I looked around, but couldn't find the other suit, "I take it he didn't survive despite that?"

"Affirmative. Pilot C-2-52 Hancha Wilka is confirmed K.I.A."

The way it said K.I.A. disgusted me. So flat, as if Hancha wasn't a human being that had a life, a family, a future. He was a conscript as well and in my unit. I was put in charge because I knew how to operate the suits somewhat better than the other conscripts in my unit since I had helped assemble them. We didn't know each other well enough to be friends, but after going through boot camp, it was hard not to form some kind of bond. I was already too numb to cry. "God, you couldn't have at least let him or someone else survive? You had to leave me with this soulless goddamn war suit?" I prayed.

No reply.

"H-How did I survive?" I asked not really caring, but just to keep making sound.

"...This suit's records were corrupted after impact... Currently processing other suit's records to make a more complete account."

"Sounds about right..." I said as I sat back down on the glass floor and stared at my suit. I had finally noticed that my stomach felt like it had a hole in it. It had been 72 hours since I ate, and all the food was stored on the N.O.F. evac ships. No rations for us. 'Either we win and the food returns, or we lose and won't need them.'

"P.A.P?"

"Affirmative. How may I assist you, pilot C-1-52?" P.A.P. repeated... Again.

"Is there a grocery store nearby?"

"Offline map data indicates there's one in Doamont city. 30 minutes walking distance from here."

"Walking? Can't I just ride you there?"

"Negative. The Rotary systems in the legs are inoperable and the city has too much debris to use treads."

"Great. Just…Great…" I sighed not looking forward to the hiking with all the bruises and aches.

"If you are in search of sustenance, please be warned: Food stored in sealed metal cans have a 70% chance of being contaminated by the U.X.C.'s toxins. All other food and water sources have a higher probability of contamination."

***

My combat boots squeaked with each step on the glassy terrain. I had to stare at the ground because I refused to look at the 'sky'. I could have sworn that I saw corpses underneath the glass in the parts not covered by the black snow. The more I tried to look at them, the more they seemed to sink away. I reached out and tried to touch a bit of the black snow out of morbid curiosity. My gloved fingers grazed it and left trails. It was packed and could be shaped, but it was warm. I had no idea what it was, but I did not want to touch it anymore.

I felt a strange relief as I entered the ruins. Under a roof, I could still pretend there was a sky and not have to see the black snow. I walked through various collapsed buildings, all caked with dust and debris. I had mentally prepared myself to see the place littered with bodies. I was more terrified to discover there weren't any. As though they had never existed. When I went deeper inside, I had to use my flashlight. With all the dust, it was like having your car's headlights in a deep fog.

My suit's map had not updated its GPS with debris in mind. That 'thirty-minute' walk turned into two hours of climbing and spelunking before I finally found the barely holding up, collapsed Walmart.

The place had been ransacked by those not lucky enough to win the Evac lottery or be wealthy and connected. They didn't get far, and what they tried to steal got damaged. There was barely anything left. Even worse, P.A.P. was right about the food. Nearly everything that wasn't canned had black pus or pulsating tumors on them. I used my combat knife to open up a can of fruit. I raised my mask slightly and held my breath as I took a mouthful and covered my face again before chewing. It tasted bitter and vial, and I enjoyed every bite of it. It was the first time I could feel something for hours, and I was overwhelmed. I finally cried as I saw the bottom of the can.

The numbness had passed, and I was alone in the darkness and silence.

I flung the can across the room in panic when I heard a muffled woman's voice coming from the manager's office. I got out my pistol in case it was the U.X.C., a looter, or something else. When I creaked open the door, I saw it was empty, but the radio was working.

"Zrrt...-9-52... Zrrt... rn Hale...No survivors... Zrrt... Away..."

52nd? Same as me. That had to mean she was nearby. I wasn't alone! I begged God to tell me I wasn't alone! I grabbed the radio and ran as fast as I could back to the suit. I had to stop more times than I'd care to admit. I would use the mask as an excuse, but my lungs were garbage. I was technically a soldier, but sitting in a cockpit all day for training didn't help with cardio.

"Pilot C-1-52, I am detecting rapid breathing and an elevating heart rate. Do you need medical treatment?" P.A.P. asked once I was back in scanning range.

"Fu... Huff... No... Huff... P.A.P. I have... Jesus... I have a radio signal."

"Affirmative. I have one as well."

I coughed a bit before asking, "What? Why didn't you say anything?"

"The transmission was only received then triangulated recently."

"Triangulated? So you know where it's coming from?"

"Affirmative. Approximately 161 clicks through the open wastes." I could have kissed her... It after hearing that.

"Hot damn! Let's get going. Open up the hatch!"

She... It did, and I climbed inside. I booted up the controls and pushed down the throttle. Then after one step, we crashed into the ground. My ears rang as glass on the ground cracked and shattered.

"Reminder Pilot C-1-52, the rotary systems in the legs are too damaged for walking." She said,

"Yep."

I engaged the tread mode, and after a bit of mechanical sliding, I was upright and driving the suit like a tank on nitrous.

The anxiety was killing me as hours went by. The drugs and adrenaline were starting to wear off. I was beginning to feel more of the pain from my injuries. Most likely exasperated due to all the climbing. The drugs were powerful stuff, and they were good stuff. We weren't allowed to get more unless P.A.P. deems it 'Vital to the mission.' It was a compromise decision by N.O.F. and M.A.I.C. since they wanted most to go to the evac shuttles. When I want more later, I can mess with some wires and fake an electrical signal to the pump inside my chest. It was a little trick we learned in boot camp to get help to survive.

Perhaps being hopped up could have been the edge we needed to win.

Or at least lose less badly. I suppose there was no point thinking about what-ifs. I had no one who I could have complained about it to, I guess. At least not at the moment. I didn't know what to say to this other person if and when I found her.

Social situations had a lot more impact when you could be one of the last people left on Earth. Would have hated for her to think she was stranded with a creep. I know I was hoping I wasn't stranded with a creep. If things had gone well, we couldn't exactly repopulate the earth. We'd have some screwed-up grandkids and even more screwed-up great-grandkids. Assuming U.X.C.'s toxins didn't make us sterile.

"Incoming missile!" P.A.P. warned.

"Jesus Christ!" I yanked the joystick off to the side and swerved as I barely avoided the missile and swung the suit back toward the assailant. The heat from the blast made me sweat in the cockpit.

"This is Pilot L-9-52 Thorn Hale of M.A.I.C. and that was a warning shot." Her voice said in my comms. "You are able to move the suit like a pilot. Are you M.A.I.C. personnel?"

"Son of- Yes I am."

"What is your designation?"

"This is Pilot C-1-52 my name is Chauffy Tre-"

"I didn't ask your name. Hold on... Designation checks out. Why did you leave your post? You were assigned to New Canonto City."

Did she not realize what happened or was she just in shock?

"I figured due to the circumstances the chain of command was Fubar... Much like everything else now."

There was a pause, but Thorn's suit had its guns trained on me. Finally, she responded, "Why did you come here?"

"I heard your signal. It wasn't very clear, but my suit managed to track it."

"I see. You obviously wouldn't have come if you heard it correctly. Good to know. I'll need to fix it. Patrol around the perimeter. Don't let anyone near the radio tower." Thorn ordered, as a practiced officer.

What? Was I supposed to go back to soldiering as if our planet wasn't glassed? As far as I was concerned, no M.A.I.C. command to threaten me meant no need to listen to their bull-crap.

"Wait, why? Don't we want other survivors to locate us?" I asked.

"This isn't broadcast for them."

My head hurt trying to figure out what she was thinking. "Who the hell is it for?"

"I'm trying to send a message to any surviving N.O.F ships to stay away."

I nearly leapt out of my seat, "Why the hell are you doing that? If there are any they can pick us up and get us off this corpse planet!"

"I won't allow it. If they are out there then they are the last surviving humans. I can't risk them coming here and being followed by the U.X.C. to kill off what's left of humanity."

I couldn't believe what she was saying. She wasn't knocked out like I was. She must have fought through this longer than I have. How could she think that? Had she gone insane?

"So-so what? Are we s-supposed to just rot here while the rich and lucky bastards get to have a luxury cruise in space?"

"We had sworn oaths to protect humanity. One life for ten." "Screw that!" I shouted, "They swore that oath for me. I'm not going to die here! I need to call for help!"

"That Oath is all that we have left. Stand down, or I will put you down!" Thorn said as her suit's weapons primed. She was a Legion Pilot of 9th rank. Not a conscript, but an honest-to-god combat veteran. Using an old comparison, if I was considered the best army grunt in terms of skill, she would be the lowest-skilled black-ops commando. Even that was more than enough to kick my ass, even without my suit being more damaged than hers. But my flight or fight instinct kicked in.

I launched all my smoke and chaff and yanked my throttle into reverse. I would not have been able to use the chaff as countermeasures against Thorn's missiles. But all the lights and smoke gave me enough time to find some cover. As my suit zig-zagged around and I looked for anything to use as cover, Thorn took blind shots at me with her railgun. The magnetically shot soda can-sized shell launched at me with lightning speed and split a broken-down semi-truck nearby just as quickly.

It was getting worse. With each shot one after another clearing up the chaff smoke, I was losing time, and there was no viable cover in sight that Thorn couldn't just punch through. Her missiles would be able to lock on, and without legs, I wouldn't have the agility to dodge them. I tried taking potshots at her, hoping I could somehow hit her with dumb luck. With each shot, I felt all my hair stand up as the rail gun charged and launched the bullet faster than any gun in the 21st century.

Either I wasn't hitting her, or she didn't care, as she didn't let up. The monitors in my cockpit alerted me that she was getting a lock on. What I was about to do was stupid as all hell, and we were told to only do this in the same scenario where shooting yourself in the head would somehow lead to victory.

"P.A.P.! Rev up the Nuclear Core!" I barked.

"Warning: with current damage to core and radiation shielding-" She warned before I used the manual override switches.

"Engaged."

Then suddenly, I nearly vomited that can of fruit as my suit drove so fast it practically glided across the ground. Thorn's missiles were locked on me, but the extra energy output made me fast enough to dodge them. She must have noticed either the radiation spike or the increased performance because her suit's Nuclear Core engaged. Only Thorn's suit could still use its legs, so she had better maneuverability. Each of Thorn's steps shattered the glass ground like an ice pick.

"You stupid son-of-a-! If you're so scared of dying, using the Nuclear Core is just going to kill you faster." Thorn shouted over the comms. I muted her. I didn't want to listen to what she was saying. Though I should have.

Despite our intense speeds, she made another shot with her railgun and blew off my missile bed. I could see light out of the hole it made in my cockpit.

I was nowhere near the marksman she was and I couldn't slow down to aim or she would make a lethal shot for sure. I was desperate and scared.

"Divert all power into the weapons system!" I ordered.

"Warning that will expose you to lethal amounts of-"

I smashed the override button. My skin started to blister and boil. I aimed the rail gun in her general direction. I charged it and nearly fried the circuits of the cockpit. Suddenly, the bullet launched out. It missed wide, but that didn't matter. The shockwave alone ripped apart her suit and it fell over. It was done, but I hoped she was still alive.

I didn't want to kill her, but I needed to leave. My suit stopped moving as it shut down. P.A.P. was dead. I used the emergency exit latch to get out of my cockpit. My insides felt like they were ripping apart, and my skin felt like the worst sunburn I've ever had. I was glad I didn't have a mirror. I imagine I didn't look so good anymore.

I went over to what was left of Thorn's cockpit, pulled open the emergency hatch, and saw that my shot took off her left arm and leg.

"You goddamn coward! You're going to finish us off!" She coughed out.

"I can't stay here," I repeated.

"And then what? Die of... agonizing radiation poisoning... in less... than a year... at best? How... could..."

She died of blood loss before she could finish. I limped to the radio, my muscles feeling weaker by the second. I croaked out, "Is anyone there… Can anyone hear this…" Silence. I fell and crawled back to my suit.

"P.A.P…. P.A.P are you alright?" She was killed in the fight.

I was all alone.

LATE GAME

It was a late Sunday night like any other. At a sports pub so cheap it was not even worth a name. The local favorite, Los Nubes Serpents, had made it to the Premier League. The television screens were flashing, and European football was playing. The torn leather seats were filling, and the frothy beer was flowing. The fans were cheering and jeering, and neither team was winning.

But one lovely lady was not here for the football or the beer. Those forms of entertainment had long lost their fascination to Cihuanen[1] for a very long time. No, her sport was hunting, and like a cat, she enjoyed playing with her food.

Like any good hunter, Cihuanen needed the proper attire. Her camouflage of choice tonight was a midnight blue velvet mini -dress, whose color could allow her to submerge into the night unseen if her trap failed to spring. The dress was alluring with its low cut and high hem, yet not so revealing as to draw the unwanted attention of the lesser game. Cihuanen wore black thigh-high boots, partially due to the rain outside, and padded to reduce the noise of her footsteps. The metal zippers were replaced with black plastic for her personal ease of use.

She painted her nails, lips, and eyes a golden shadow complimenting her deep bronze complexion, amber-brown eyes, and long curly chestnut hair. In Cihuanen's mortal youth, this lack of paint and color would have been dull, at best, compared to what she wore in ceremonial occasions such as this. But times have changed, and standing out too much was dangerous for a hunter like her. The only thing she wore from her home was her round turquoise earrings held up by a high-quality plastic post.

1 Cihuanen - A name. Pronounced See-Huwan-En.

Her prey this month was a man. Her kind, the Tlahuelpuchi[2], usually hunted children, but for Cihuanen, it lacked sportsmanship. It couldn't be just any man, though. It would be too easy for a beautiful woman like her to lure a dazzled drunk back to her place. She tried to find the outliers, the unique, the standouts, or the outcasts. The ones lesser skilled hunters ignored. Someone deserving yet with enough skepticism not to be fooled by her traps so easily. Only one man was worthy to hunt tonight.

"Good evening, handsome. Which team are you rooting for?" Cihuanen asked as she sat on the stool between her prey and another lesser man who was typing on his phone. Her voice was warm and pleasing to get his attention away from the undrunken shot glass he had been staring at for an hour.

"W-what? Oh, I-I'm sorry. I-I didn't..." He said, startled. He had short jet-black hair and big watery blue eyes hidden behind glasses that studied Cihuanen with wonder. His face was young. With a strong, clean-shaven jaw. He looked tired. So very tired. He wore a soft oak-colored shirt jacket that hugged around him and jeans that were tight in places Cihuanen enjoyed.

His face was freckled and pale until it flushed after Cihuanen asked, "Do you like what you see?"

"I-I am so sorry. Your- your earrings. They're beautiful."

"Oh, thank you," Cihuanen replied, a little surprised. It usually wasn't the first thing people noticed about her, but she wasn't after the usual. She wanted to see how far she could test him. With a graceful movement, she moved the stool over, deliberately narrowing the gap between them until they were intimately close.

"You may call me Cihuanen. Are you enjoying the game alone?" She asked with playful intrigue.

His shaky hand adjusted his glasses, clearly trying not to look below her eyes, "I-I guess so." The surrounding boos from disgruntled patrons over a referee's call emphasized his nervousness.

"How lovely. It seems I have the pleasure of your exclusive company tonight."

"Martin! My-my name is Martin. Nice to meet you." He stammered. Beads of sweat were forming on Martin's neck as he reached out his hand for a shake. Cihuanen decided to ease off a little. Let him recover some confidence lest she spooked him away and shook it like a professional greeting.

---

2 Tlahuelpuchi - A mythological creature. Pronounced T'la-h'well'poochi

"Can I help you with anything?" Martin asked so genuinely Cihuanen thought it was cute, like a deer eating food out of the palm of its predator.

"I'm just looking for fun. What do you do for fun?" She asked, getting him to focus on his hobbies now instead of his nervousness.

"I-I'm a football coach for students of low-income families. It's not particularly exciting, I know. It pays next to nothing."

"Pay isn't everything. As long as you enjoy what you do."

"I know. Life forces those kids to grow up too fast. I know they gotta support their families, but is it too much to ask that children should enjoy childhood?" Martin said before bashfully sitting back down as the other man, who sat on the stool behind Cihuanen, rolled his eyes before returning to his phone.

"Ignore him. What you do is great. More people need to accept the honesty of their passions." Cihuanen said, repeating some old wisdom of her mother's.

"What about you? What's your passion?" Martin asked, which Cihuanen assumed was a subtle test to see if her interest in him was for 'financial' reasons.

"I trade equity in Platinum." Though, she would never touch the stuff.

"Ooh, interesting! Why Platinum? Isn't Gold a better trade option?" It's always about Gold for men like them, isn't it? It was because of Gold they ravaged her homeland. It was because of Gold that they scoured the American West. When they eventually traded with paper, it still represented Gold. They only stopped using the Gold Standard because, as always, they could never get enough Gold. Even Los Nubes Serpents wore Gold as the color of their uniforms. What better way to lure men like them than to paint herself in Gold? Paint herself in the very thing they crossed oceans, jungles, and mountains to find.

"Too many people discard the value of Platinum, so I swooped in and took advantage. I don't know if I would call that my passion. It doesn't burn in me like my past passion." Back when she hunted those who destroyed her homeland and every one of their descendants. These days there are none left by blood, but she could always find them in spirit. Even if she had to look harder and stretch out her search.

"What happened?" Martin asked.

"I don't want to talk about it," Cihuanen said curtly, knowing that Martin meant nothing by it and had no reason to suspect her, but her old defensive instincts kicked in.

"Understood, sorry. Um, what do you do for fun?"

"I like to go hunting occasionally." Though these days, it was becoming more out of habit. And to stave off boredom.

"Oh, that's cool! My dad and I used to go deer hunting every winter. What kind of game do you go after?"

Realizing Martin was distracted the way she intended, it was time to swoop in again, "Large and dangerous game," she purred, her tone laced with a hint of mischief. "The kind that gets your heart pumping. Maybe I can show you some of the trophies at my place tonight?" She asked, tilting her head and slightly exposing her smooth neck.

"Y-you're very forward, aren't you?" Martin chuckled nervously while the Serpants'coach was on screen giving one of his players the hairdryer treatment.

"Is that a bad thing?" She teased, leaning ever so closer to him. "No, not at all! It's good that you're so confident. It's just a bad time for me." Martin said, looking back at his undrunken glass.

A vulnerability? Yes, Cihuanen could use that. Provide a little... nudge.

"Perhaps I can help you instead?"

At the moment, Martin's face was almost as crimson as Patecatl[3]. Cihuanen had to stifle a laugh as Martin stuttered, "I-I-I... Look. You seem so nice and smart and interesting and gorgeous- Uh. Uh. I'm so sorry I didn't-"

"No, no. Keep going; I want to hear more." Cihuanen sighed sweetly. She had won the game now, or she thought. Martin turned to his undrunken glass. His eyes reddened until tears started leaking out.

Something was definitely wrong. Cihuanen hadn't planned for this. What does she do now?

"I I'm sorry. I just... I just had a horrible breakup and... I don't know how I am feeling... and I don't want someone as... As captivating as you to feel... feel like I am using you for a rebound."

Martin's hands were trembling around the glass.

"What happened?" Cihuanen asked, startled at her own flash of sincerity. It was unfamiliar territory.

Martin let himself breathe for a moment. He let the emotions in, then let them pass through him, "I don't know. We had been with each other for almost ten years since high school. I tried proposing to her, but she said no, so I thought she wasn't ready, and I didn't want to push her. Thought she just needed more time..." His voice wavers again as the emotions overwhelm him, "But then, one day, all her stuff was gone from our apartment. She didn't even leave a note. I had to find out through a Facebook post that she left me for someone more exciting."

3 Patecatl - A mythological god. Pronounced Pate-catl.

Cihuanen remembered that sorrow. It was an old memory she had smothered with absolute wrath so corrosive it killed. Yet Martin was not feeling fury nor ire. Not even outrage at the betrayal and abandonment. Just… Grief.

"Why?" Cihuanen asked coldly.

"What?" Martin asked, calming down and wiping his eyes with a napkin on the table.

"Why are you not angry? Why are you not lashing out at them?" Cihuanen's voice rose out of her control.

"What good would that do?"

"It would serve as a lesson. Make them regret hurting you in the first place!" Wasn't that obvious? She thought.

"But she was already gone. Lashing out won't bring her back. If I harmed either of them, would I be any better?"

"I-" She felt her throat tightening. What is this? Her fingers twirled her soft hair. Was she feeling nervous? Her heart was beating slightly faster. Why? Martin was no threat. He was too gentle, too considerate, and too- Wait! Was she worried about what he thought of her?

"I-I," Cihuanen tried again. This was ridiculous. She barely knew him. Yet she wanted to know more, wanted to know everything about him.

Oh no, this wasn't good; her trap had malfunctioned. How can Martin be so in control of his lust and anger? How can he be okay with feeling sorrow? Why was Cihuanen getting so bothered by this feeling that she was yearning? She was losing control of both herself and the situation. She needed to regain her composure and leave, or else this would get frightening.

"Do you want anything, Ma'am?" The bartender asked.

"Pulque![4]" Cihuanen demanded automatically. She wasn't sure why she even ordered anything. Her kind is immune to poison. It wouldn't have calmed her nerves.

"I've never heard of Pulque before. Where is it from?" Martin asked.

"My homeland," Cihuanen responded, her knee bobbing impatiently for the drink so she could leave.

"I was wondering, where are you from? I've never heard an accent like yours before."

"I think you would call it Mexico City." She answered while refusing to look at him. She had never returned home. Not since her mother tongue was no longer the lingua franca.

---

4   Pulque - An alcoholic drink made by fermenting sap from the maguey. Pronounced Pull-k.

"Oh, you don't sound Spanish."

"I'm not," She said coldly, feeling insulted at the comparison of the conquerors. She wanted to shut him up but craved the sound of his voice.

"Oh, sorry, I shouldn't have assumed."

Cihuanen was losing her patience with his courtesy and apologies. It had to be fake. She was looking for a deer to kill and found a mockingbird imitating its call. Martin was just annoying to her now, she was telling herself. She would find someone else to hunt and forget this embarrassing mistake ever happened.

The bartender handed Cihuanen her off-white drink, and Martin raised his glass to her.

"I guess here's to making new friends, huh?"

"I'm not looking for friends,"

"Well, if you ever need one," Martin said before finally taking a drink from his shot glass.

Cihuanen took a sip. The Pulque was just like she remembered. Viscous, sweet, and zingy. A Mi'totiliztli[5] dance on her tongue. Perhaps she ordered it as a comfort drink, something to center herself if nothing else, or maybe it was an unexpected pang of nostalgia.

She placed it down behind her as Martin started coughing, "I guess it would have been better when it was cold." He said while chuckling.

Despite the ever-loudening crowd of sports fans booing at the missed shot, Cihuanen barely heard a plopping sound followed by the squeaking chair of the lesser man on his way out of the pub.

How droll. That pathetic man thought he could roofie her? He was a kitten who believed he could hunt a Jaguar. Nothing more.

Cihuanen reached for her drink again, but Martin stopped her. "Woah! Did that guy just spike your drink?" Martin whispered to her. Cihuanen was in no danger due to her immunity, yet she played along,

"I think so. I don't feel safe here anymore. Could you walk me home, please? In case he tries to follow me."

"O-of course!" Martin said, then informed the bartender of what happened and tried to give a detailed description of the unsavory man. As they were on their way out, a roar of cheers filled the pub as the game went into extra time, giving Los Nubes Serpents a chance to win at the last minute.

***

What the hell was Cihuanen doing? She wanted to get away from Martin, yet she couldn't seem to pull herself from him. The relentless

---

5 Mi'totiliztli - Pronounced Mee-to-til-iz-tli.

rain would not have bothered her since she couldn't get cold or sick, yet she clung to him under his umbrella as if the water were acidic. She would have laughed if she wasn't so humiliated and terrified of what she was feeling.

"H-here, why don't you take my jacket?" Martin asked as they went through a crosswalk. The streetlight overhead gave his face an emerald glow. She had forgotten how to respond.

"Please, I insist. You're shaking." Of course, she was. Yet, another thing to add to her mortification.

"Oh." Was all Cihuanen could squeeze out of her dry throat. She didn't need it, yet she didn't resist as he gently placed it around her bare shoulders. It was soft, fuzzy, and warm like a blanket and had the unmistakable scent of Cypress trees. The smell seemed to be the only thing calming her, so she brought the collar to her face and inhaled greedily.

When she was willing to relinquish her breath, she glanced back at Martin. The humidity made his stone grey tee shirt cling to his broad chest and shoulders. When their eyes met, Cihuanen became acutely aware of what she was doing. Her face felt hot, and she did not appreciate the role reversal of embarrassment. She averted her eyes back down but noticed an imprint on his chest that provoked her.

"Are you religious?" Cihuanen asked, just barely keeping her voice from showing her contempt.

"Why do you- Oh, this," Martin said as he untucked a necklace from his shirt. A Gold crucifix.

Of course, that had to be it, the anxiousness and the inability to let him go despite wanting to get away from him earlier. Cihuanen knew she couldn't have picked the wrong prey. She never had before. Martin was simply more clever than the others. The politeness, sincerity, and openness? It must have been his camouflage. Her body just reacted instinctively even when her mind didn't. That must have been it. He was like the Spaniards, using their beliefs for their selfish gain. A smile came to her lips as she finally had confirmation, yet she didn't feel relieved like she thought she would.

"Not really. It belonged to my dad. He gave it to me when I was eight before he died of cancer. My mother was inconsolable, so I had to take care of everything. I moved out as soon as I could because I realised that was no way for a kid to live. No matter where I went. Or what I lost, I kept this with me."

Was Cihuanen wrong? Was this the first time, or had she been trying to reinforce her beliefs before? Cihuanen rubbed her fingers across her turquoise earrings anxiously. She was twelve when her parents discovered what she was. They protected her secret out of shame and fear of what the other dignitaries would do to her. But she knew they still loved her despite her horrific needs. When the Conquistadors murdered her parents, instead of waiting for the fire to die down and collect their ashes, Cihuanen spread the flames so the monsters and their spawn would burn too.

"I wish I still had something from my parents. They've been gone for a very, very long time." Cihuanen wasn't sure why she said that, but she was happy she told him.

When they reached the apartment building, Martin opened the door for her, and halfway in, she stopped and faced him.

"I think your ex chose poorly."

"What do you mean?" He asked, cocking his brow.

"Exciting is fun and all, but only kindness ever seems to last."

"Th-thanks."

Their eyes connected once more. Neither wanted to look away this time. The rain continued to beat on, and on, and on the umbrella.

"It-it was nice meeting you," Martin said, breaking the silence.

"Come inside," Cihuanen said. Ready to beg for him.

"Are you sure?"

"Please."

***

Cihuanen unlocked her apartment and turned on the lights with her phone as the two walked inside. It was a two-story penthouse with an open view of the city. In her few quiet moments, she would stay up all night and watch the neon lights dance below. Inside, the apartment was full of luxuries that not even the kings of her time could fathom. Renowned artisans meticulously handcrafted each piece of furniture. She gave them all the funding they needed to make each one a masterpiece, from her bed to the tables, to the chairs and couches, and even to the carpet that lines the floors. Historical pieces, artifacts, and treasures from around the world nearly half a millennia old lined her walls in ornamental glass displays that are never touched.

Cihuanen never showed any of them off. She never had friends over. The very few who saw them were her victims. And they didn't live long enough to see them all. It was a final mockery to the Conquistadors. While they hounded endlessly and committed atrocities to find their imaginary 'El Dorado,' she made her home more priceless than any city of Gold could hope to be. When Cihuanen saw it now, it all looked gaudy and pointless to her.

"Wow… How can I get into the Platinum market?" Martin joked as he spun around to see as much as he could.

"A little late to the game, I'm afraid. It's slim pickings now." Cihuanen chuckled.

"Damn. Just missed it, didn't I?" By a few hundred years, but his grin persisted.

"No way are those real? Where are they from?" Martin asked as he pointed to the rows of helmets.

"Everything here is. Those were from Spain. I used to collect those." As well as the heads that once adorned them, they had decayed into nothingness over time, as she had not taken any steps to preserve them.

While Martin bounced around, looking at each display like a child in a candy store, Cihuanen searched through her vinyl records like leafing through a dictionary. When she found the one she wanted, Cihuanen pulled the disc from the poly-lined inner sleeve and set it on her record player. She turned it on, and as soon as the needle dropped, Edith Piaf sang through the room.

Cihuanen grabbed Martin's hand and pulled him toward her before he could admire another piece. He was caught off guard by her strength but enjoyed the embrace.

"Wouldn't you much rather look my way?" Cihuanen asked, her hips swaying with the music as her lips hovered over his.

"Y-you just went through a scary moment with the perv spiking your drink. I-I don't want to take advantage of you."

"You won't take advantage of me." Her lips crept closer. "I don't want you to ever worry about being a rebound."

"I won't. I trust you." And even though she didn't know it yet, it was true. She moved his hands ever lower down her back.

"Are you-Are you sure?"

"It's what I've wanted all night," Cihuanen whispered as her lips finally pressed against his. The skin on her lower back tingled, her breath forced its way in, and her heart threatened to beat out her chest. She had kissed many times before, but this truly felt like her first.

***

They didn't reach the bedroom, which was most likely a good thing. The bed no longer felt genuine to Cihuanen. Although, the floor wasn't exactly the most comfortable sleeping choice. Martin made for a conveniently cozy pillow. He was still asleep. The throw blanket couldn't cover his bare chest, and Cihuanen placed the fingertips of both her hands in the center.

With a tiny push, Cihuanen could open up to his heart and fill herself with his blood.

"It is I, the Tlahuelpuchi. Pay attention, brother heart, who is sustenance." Her throat was catching, but she continued the prayer, "Pay attention, Mixcoatl[6], for now, I entrust into your hands my… My prey, the one who gives us or the one who is our sustenance." Repeating the words she has recited so many times before.

Her stomach was ravenous, and her mouth watered. She had to do this. It was not malicious, it was survival. If she didn't do this every month she would starve. Martin would understand if he knew right? He cared for her. Like no one has ever cared for her. And that's why she couldn't do it. After everything she… She couldn't. Cihuanen gently moved her hands to Martin's warm cheeks and kissed him over and over till he woke.

"Good evening, handsome. Or I guess good morning now." She said, smiling.

"Good morning. Are you alright?" Martin asked groggily.

Cihuanen wiped a tear from her eye, "I'm fine. I just forgot to get groceries recently and was going to get some food." There were plenty of other predators out in the city besides her. Perhaps the imbecile who spiked her drink could make for a quick meal?

"Do you want me to get you anything to eat?"

"Yeah, sure. That would be nice." Martin said.

Cihuanen threw on some comfortable clothes, attempting to ignore her hunger pains as she 'borrowed' Martin's shirt jacket. Martin turned on the tv, getting himself to wake up. Apparently, Los Nubes Serpents lost to Feathered Flores in the final seconds. Nobody seemed to believe they could lose after such a long streak.

"Cihuanen?" Martin called as she was putting on her shoes.

"Yes?"

"Well, uh… Thank you. For everything."

She nodded, and just before she closed the door,

"Martin?" "What's up?"

"I wouldn't mind being your friend." And perhaps something more?

6 Mixcoatl - A mythological god. Pronounced M-ee-z-kh-ah-t-l.

PERPETUAL PICTURES

Eric took an agonizing, gurgling breath as his blunt continued to burn up to his fingertips. Despite the pain, he held it tightly as though it were his last grasp of life. The foul aroma, once a source of calm and comfort, was the final feeling of pain he would ever experience again.

And it was slow. Slower than anything Eric had ever experienced. Slow as infinity but most assuredly approaching. There was nothing that could be done. He was done.

"Is it worse being high? Or am I lucky?" Eric wondered in brief bits of clarity.

The crackling, chaotic illumination from his secondhand television began to dim. The political newscasters endlessly argued about issues that would never be resolved. Only pausing to advertise luxuries Eric would never own.

"Why did I ever care?" He asked himself, knowing now that he wouldn't live to see the consequences while hoping they would not harm him in the next life.

All light retreated from him. Fluttering away like fireflies no longer within reach. Like falling slowly down a deep, dark well.

"Was it always so beautiful?" Eric wondered before his brain ran out of oxygen to think.

His lungs forced another breath, choking him on his own blood as it began to fill like water balloons soon to pop. The soft, warm, fuzzy carpet Eric took naps on after wild parties of drinking and smoking began to feel cold as a block of ice as hours drifted past.

His insides were scrambled by the bullet that forced its way into his gut and out his back. His ears still rang from the gunshot like a choir forever singing the final note. Eric either closed his eyes or finally lost his vision. It didn't matter. He was comforted in believing, in knowing, that he would start again even if he wouldn't remember it.

***

Eric regained consciousness. He was still... Himself? He had not expected that. Did he somehow survive? Eric was no doctor, but he frankly couldn't see how. The pain was gone, but he could hear muffled sounds around him. Although Eric was ready, he supposed it wasn't such a bad thing to still be alive.

After sleeping off the drugs, Eric could see his girlfriend again. After experiencing near death, proposing to her didn't seem so frightening anymore. Yet Eric couldn't sleep. He wasn't tired like before when he had his tonsils removed. Eric didn't feel the tingling numbness painkillers gave. Not even the slightest hint of high from the weed he smoked before all of this.

It was nothingness. No comfort or discomfort. Eric forced himself to open his eyes and saw he was still at his apartment. Or at least he thought it was. Everything was wispy and nearly devoid of all color except one. It was as if he wore blue-tinted drunk goggles.

"What the hell?" Eric heard his voice say. Surprised he could speak at all, considering his lungs were full of blood, last he remembered.

Police tape hung everywhere like tasteless curtains. Forensic photographers took pictures of his apartment, similar to tourists in a museum while cops searched for something. All of whom appeared blue and blurred like a camera out of focus.

"Hey! What are you all doing? Is nobody going to help? I'm dying over here!" Eric shouted indignantly, but none of the police officers paid him any attention.

"You ain't dying, kid. You're dead." said a deep voice with a strange accent from across the room.

Eric followed the voice and saw some middle-aged man in a worn-out trench coat his grandfather would have worn. He, too, was blue. It was hard to see his detailed features, but the man was more in focus than everyone else in the room. Perhaps because he was crouching right next to him?

"What's going on? And why is everything so goddamn blue?"

"Looks blue to you, huh? Us folk my age see it all black and white like in them pictures. Must be how we's thinking it ought to be." The older man said as if they were having a casual conversation about the weather.

"What are you talking about?" Eric asked, not bothering to hide his frustration.

"Look down, kid." He said as he pointed.

Eric almost refused to do so until he got some answers. But morbid curiosity won. He gazed below. Eric was sitting inside a bleeding body.

"Jesus Christ!" Eric screamed as he jumped up and realized it was his body lying there.

"Haven't crossed paths with the guy. Can't say if I ever will anymore. You can bet your bottom dollar I's got an earful to give him if I do."

"What did you do to me?" Eric felt like he was going to vomit, but nothing was coming out.

"Calm down, kid. Worrying ain't going to do yous any good." "Get the hell away from me, you sick son-of-a-!" Eric swung his fist at the man. Whatever happened must have made Erice more disoriented than he thought. His fist flew right through the man's face while he stared unflinchingly.

"Yous done yet?"

"I need to call my girlfriend!" Eric squeaked out.

"Good luck with that." He said, rolling his eyes.

Eric ignored him and tried reaching for the phone in his pocket, only for his hand to clip through his blue leg. He repressed that bit of terror and concluded that it must still be in his body's pocket. He tried to reach in there and screamed as his hand went through one end of the leg and out the other.

"Pipe down, kid! You'll wake the dead... Heheh."

"This can't be happening, I must be having a fever dream or something. Right?" Eric asked, looking back at the older man.

"Hold on. Detectives arrivin' on scene."

Eric watched as a man and woman in sharply dressed suits approached one of the officers.

"The vic was a college student. Twenty-three years old. According to the landlord, his name was Eric Roberts. Time of death was estimated to be twenty minutes ago, but neighbors reported hearing the gunshot four hours prior. Classic bystander effect occurred. No one called until it was too late." The officer told them.

"Four hours! Those assholes let me bleed out for four hours!"

"Yeah that's a rough one. Judging by the hole in your old gut it looks like it was... Eh, I think a ten-millimeter hollow point. Fired right about..." The older man stood with the television six feet to his left and the couch two feet to his right before aiming his finger pistols five feet from where Eric had stood, "Heres..." Eric shifted uncomfortably at the accuracy of the older man's recreation.

"Eh. Sorry. Hope it didn't hurt too bad." The older man said, scratching the back of his head.

"I... Who-who are you?" Eric asked.

"Former Detective Jim Waller. Nice to meet yous." Jim said, reaching out for a handshake.

Eric tried to shake it, but his hand went through his. "Am I dead?"

"Yep," Jim said, then went right back to looking around the apartment.

"What are we doing here?"

"I assume you was livin here."

"I mean why am I still," Eric waved his arms around, "Here and not somewhere else?"

"Well, kid, you look like you just kicked the bucket, so you probably haven't gotten very far from your cadaver. Me? Well, solvin' murders' was what I did for a livin'. While I was still livin', mind you. So I turned it into a pastime now that I'm one of the murdered ones. Helps kill time, you know. No pun intended."

Eric tried to process all of this. His heart should have been racing, his face hot and sweaty, but nothing. He could feel the emotions but not the bodily responses that came with them. That alone was unnerving, to say the least.

"Were you watching me the whole time?"

Jim laid down staring intensely at the crime scene outline as he answered, "Nope. I's just got here when I heard the sirens."

Eric sat on the floor, not wanting to risk falling through any of the chairs. The fuzzy carpet didn't feel warm or cold to him anymore.

"So I'm really dead?"

Jim gave a look of disbelief as he asked, "Hearin it three times ain'ts enough?"

"No reincarnation?"

"Don't think so."

"Is this Hell?"

"If it is, it's not what I was told it was like in Sunday school so until proven otherwise I'mma goin with no." Jim said, angling his head toward where a pile of philosophy textbooks were knocked over by the killer.

Eric looked at his wispy fingers. Unable to touch anything. Unable to hold anyone. "So there's no place we go to when we die? It's just... Nothing?"

"Not as fars as I can tell. Though, I's wouldn't call this nothin' either. Sure as hell beats oblivion, if I's say so."

"And you're dead too?"

"Last I checked." Jim answered as he ran back and forth, tracing the steps of where the killer left the scene.

"How did you die?"

"What's it to yous?"

"I... I don't know. I guess I just need to talk."

Jim sighed, annoyed to pause his investigation. "I was doin' my job, see? Chasin' a slimy speakeasy owner down an alley. He turned his heels, pulled out a swiped army M1911. A bigol' bang got me. Thought he missed as I was still hot on his heels, but then I's heard a thud behind me. I slammed on my brakes and there I am. My own body, lying theres like a lost button on my jacket."

Eric tried to avoid looking at his own body, pretending it wasn't there.

"I can't believe this." Eric said mostly to himself.

"Believe or don't believe, it is what it is."

Eric crawled to his knees, "Please let me go back! My girlfriend, my family. I can't- I can't leave them like this."

"Theres ain't no going back, kid."

"Please! I'll do anything!" "I ain't the

one to talk to."

"Who is?" Tears should have swum out of Eric's eyes, but nothing came.

"I's don't know, so quit asking!" Jim huffed, "Look, kid, the only way to talk to thems again is to wait till they kick the bucket too. I don't make the rules."

Eric balled his fists and seethed through his breath.

"Then we need to catch Michael Sompton! That asshole killed me because he thought I snitched on him and got him expelled!"

Jim made a slapping motion on his knee and his hand passed through it, "Now why did yous have to tell me the ending of the book while I was in the middle of reading it?"

"This is my life or death or whatever! I'm not some goddamn mystery novel!" Eric made the motion of ripping down his bookshelf, but nothing happened, "Are you going to help me find him or what?"

"Say I do help yous, and say yous do find him. Then what? What do you think yous can do in your current state?" Jim asked, arms outstretched.

"I don't know. Freaking haunt his ass or something."

"Oh yeah, good use of eternity. Stalk a guy for sixty some years until he dies of old age. Maybe make his spine tingle a little once inna blue moon."

"So I should just give up then? Just sit here forever?" Eric sighed as he let his fists relax.

Jim sat beside him, "No, don't throws in the towel just yet. Yous gotta understand, guys like us can't change something like this anymore. They're outta our hands this side of the fence. But yous got all the time in the world to change other things. Pick up a hobby, learn a new lingo, or do anything you can to keep the motor running."

"That's bullcrap! None of this is fair!" Eric tried to slam his fist on the ground, but pulled his hand back at the last second. He did not want to see it go through the floor.

"Now don't go all ginger-snap on me. I've been here since the nineteen fifties and yous don't hear me complaining. What year is it now, by the way?"

"The twenty-twenties."

Jim started to laugh as he said, "You're shitting me! Damn, my ex could be afta me like a bat out of hell any minute now. She ain't too happy I's died so soon afta the divorce and no longer had to pay alimony, see? Why don't we's hide at the matinee and catch a picture? Best seats forever now."

Eric let out a breath before saying, "Sure, whatever. I suppose I need a little break after all of this."

***

Jim had to help Eric on his way to the movie theater as Eric had only ever driven there and didn't know the way by foot. Considering his current spectral circumstances, a car was no longer an option. His feet couldn't hurt anymore, so distance would never bother him. They were slowed down by Eric's old habit of waiting for traffic signals and looking both ways before crossing a street.

"Cars can't kills yous no more fussbudget," Jim said, getting impatient with Eric and walking right in the middle of ongoing traffic as cars went right through him to illustrate the point.

Eric followed, but couldn't help reflexively wincing and ducking as he saw headlights coming straight at him.

It took half an hour to reach the theater. It was the graveyard shift by the time they arrived for the very late-night movie watchers.

"Any movie you wanted to watch?" Eric asked.

"Not really. I stopped understandin' a lotta these afta the seventies. Everythin' moves too fast in'em and the plots get ridiculous. Can't keeps up."

Eric looked at the showtimes and picked a rom-com that he and his girlfriend had planned to see. Those plans were probably canceled now.

"How long will I have to wait before she can see me?" Eric wondered as he waited in line at the concession stand. It took him a moment to remember no one could see him so he tried and failed to scoop up some popcorn himself before he also remembered he couldn't eat.

"Yous really not gettin' the whole dead thing are yous?" Jim chuckled out.

"I- Old habits…" Eric said defeatedly. Feeling like a heathen for going to the theater without popcorn.

There were a few young couples inside the auditorium, but other than them it was rather empty. Jim had picked the back row and sat down.

"How are you doing that? Can we sit in chairs?"

"Only if yous thinks you can." Jim said, reclining back and stretching his arms.

"What do you mean?"

"Well let's just say there's a bit of mind over matter involved. Just don't thinks too hard about it or else you'lls fall through the floor. Lost a few wise guys that way."

"I see," Eric said, refusing to look at the ground now.

It was hard for Eric to see the movie itself through all the wispy blue haze and his mind raced too much with questions and concerns for him to pay attention to the dialogue.

"So does everyone who dies turn into a ghost?" Eric asked.

"You don't need to whisper, kid. And yes as far as I can tell."

"Then where is everyone? Millions of living things die every day and the Earth has been around for billions of years. Shouldn't there be ghosts everywhere?" Eric asked, noticing the absence.

"Right to the hard questions eh?" Jim said, trying to loosen his tie, but his hand went right through it.

"Ya notice how ever since you cashed your chips it's been real hazy? Like walking into a smoking bar that's on fires?"

"Yeah?" Eric answered, not knowing where this was going.

"Well, that's… It's a… The thing is… Eternity's a real long stretch. I mean it. A real. Long. Stretch. It's a whole lotta time where we're kinda… Stuck, just watchin' the show. Some folk… Eh they just calls it quits afta a while. Once theys realize that's all theres is. They just stop movin' like theys turned into potted plants or somethin'."

"I guess… I became Buddhist so I thought I would reincarnate. Hoped my next life would be better." Eric wished he had his prayer beads now. Even though, as being a ghost showed, it wouldn't solve his problem, the feeling of them between his fingers would have been comforting.

"I was Catholic and thought I'd be seeing the pearly gates. Looks like we're both shit outta luck here. It's a good thing yous ain't one-a-them holier-than-thou types though. Those who put all their eggs in the holy basket take it the worst. When they find out all their piety ain't worth a hill of beans in the grand scheme of things, forget about it. Now do that for a gazillion and some souls who can waltz right through each other, and it gets hazy. In some spots, you can't even see the nose on your face. It's that crowded. You're seein' me 'cause it's a bit clearer here, and I'm movin' around, ya see?

Eric was hyperventilating, but since he no longer breathed, it was more accurate to say he was pantomiming hyperventilation. He wasn't walking alone for eternity, he was swimming in an ocean of trillions of catatonic souls and counting. How long until he fades and becomes part of the scenery? How long until he loses all sense of self? How long until his mind is as dead as his body?

"Sorry, kid. I knows it's a lot to take in. But yous get used to it."

"How the hell am I supposed to get used to wandering for eternity until I go insane!" Eric shot up from his chair.

"I don't know! But yous gotta do something!" Jim snapped back. He took a breath and continued, "Look, kid, just think about thems pictures there. Sure we would all like to crack cases with Glenn Ford or swipe a smooch from Grace Kelly, but all we can do is sit here and watch some other schmuck do 'em. But you know what? That ain't such a bad deal though. We get a real kick watchin their adventures on the big screen. Hell, we even pluck down a solid fifty cents to catch these flicks."

A chuckle threatened to creep into Eric. Hard to imagine a time movies only charged fifty cents when popcorn alone was over fifteen dollars these days.

"And the best part? Showbiz keeps churning out new ones! You get the occasional fresh story, the real classy lookin' actors and actresses, and jaw-dropping new fangled effects that knock your socks off! And guys like us, we get to have the best seats in the house."

A smile finally debuted since Eric's death. "I thought you couldn't understand a lot of the movies from the past since the seventies?"

"I'ms bein' metaphorical, you nincompoop. Evens if I can't follow these new crazy plots, I's can still enjoy the spectacle."

"Sorry… Thank you, for what you said… It's assuring in a way." Jim hovered his hand over Eric's shoulder. "Ah, forget about it, kid. At the end of the day, we might be pushin' daisies, but the world ain't gonna stop spinning any time soon and while it does, might as well enjoy the latest pictures."

HARRY HAWTHORN V. HIS CHARACTERS

Eight-thirty AM. The recently conceived courthouse is packed to the brim. The defendant, Harry Hawthorn, sits nervously in his chair. His hands shake from caffeine withdrawal.

Harry was escorted to trial in an abrupt fashion and wasn't given enough time to dress formally. He wears a lizard green turtleneck sweater, a pair of shorts, and a fedora. His long, dark, graying beard and mustache are unkempt and lacking the usual pomade, and his brown eyes are still red from the blunt he had a few hours before.

The prosecutor, in contrast, wears an expensive suit perfectly tailored to him. His blonde hair is short and slick, and his face is flawlessly clean-shaven almost to a shine. His bright sapphire eyes blaze with vindictive determination. The prosecutor stands in immaculate posture as he straightens his papers in a satisfying parallel while the Judge gets to his bench.

"Please rise. The Court of the First Literary Circuit, Criminal Division, is now in session. The Honorable Judge Albert is presiding." The bailiff says. His appearance matches precisely how you imagine a background character would.

"Everyone but the jury may be seated." Judge Albert says, then turns to the bailiff, "Mr. Umm?"

"I guess just call me John, your honor." John, the just now named bailiff, says.

"Very well, John. Please swear in the jury."

"Please raise your right hand." John, the bailiff orders, and the Jury does so. Each juror has a blending into the background effect from where they came from. But when they all sit next to each other, from such unique places, it turns them into a colorful cast.

"Do you solemnly swear or affirm that you will listen to this case and render a true verdict and a fair sentence as to the defendant?" The Jury says yes. Some are in their own languages but are somehow understood by each other.

"You may be seated." And the jury does.

Judge Albert raises his high-pitched voice so it can echo in the courtroom, "Members of the jury, your duty today will be to determine the defendant, Mr. Hawthorn's guilt, or lack thereof, based only on facts and evidence provided in this case. The prosecution must prove beyond reasonable doubt that a crime was committed and that the defendant is the person who committed the crime. If he cannot, then the defendant must be found not guilty. Today's case is Harry Hawthorn versus his characters. Is the prosecution ready?"

The prosecutor stands without a single wrinkle in his suit, "Yes, your honor." And sits back down.

"Is the defense ready?" Judge Albert asks.

"Where is my attorney? I can't reach mine since I don't have any service wherever the… this place is. I should at least have a public defender given to me. Ius ad attornatus, your honor." Harry says, hoping that his use of legal Latin will impress the Judge and jury.

Judge Albert adjusts his half-moon glasses as he says, "Unfortunately, your public attorney was murdered in your work-in-progress crime thriller novel, and you have yet to reveal his killer's identity. Due to the supernatural circumstances that allowed this trial and the lack of other legal characters at our disposal, the court has decided it would present a conflict of interest if you were allowed to write in a new lawyer. So you will have to defend yourself."

"What kind of kangaroo crap court is this?" Harry shouted.

Judge Albert wiggles his gavel, "I understand your frustration. But the court insists that the defendant refrain from vulgar language or be held in contempt."

"How can this be a fair trial?"

"Mr. Hawthorn, although I find these unorthodox methods distasteful as well. We must partake in them for this trial to proceed. The characters must be allowed to have their own voice as this matter greatly concerns them. You can rest assured that I am an impartial Judge since you wrote me that way. Now, is the defense ready?"

"Do I have a choice?"

The prosecutor gives Harry a smug grin that reveals his almost reflective straight white teeth while he says, "No, you do not."

"Unfortunately, due to the short form length allotted to us, the prosecutor is correct. The people you have written demand answers. We have to provide it here and now. Mr. Stu, are you ready to make your opening statement?"

"Indeed I am, your honor. May I step into the well?" Mr. Stu, the prosecutor, asks.

"You may." Judge Albert nods.

"Thank you." Mr. Stu casually steps into the well and looks around the court, like browsing for a third sports car. "Your Honor, members of the jury. I am representing every single character the defendant has written and, if allowed to continue, will write." Mr. Stu projects his voice, making it sound like a thunderous decree, "I intend to prove that Harry Hawthorn has committed multiple degrees of assault, murder, kidnapping, negligence, enslavement, torture both physical and psychological, and many other depraved crimes that my witnesses and evidence shall prove to the jury beyond any doubt. Once you have seen them all, please find Harry Hawthorn guilty of the charges. Thank you."

"Mr. Hawthorn, how do you plea?"

"Obviously not guilty, your honor," Harry says with indignation. "This is all preposterous slander… Or would it be libel here? Either way I am a pacifist and low down on anyone who uses violence of any sort."

"Very well. The prosecution may begin direct examination."

Mr. Stu turns to Judge Albert, "Thank you, your Honor. I call Witness One to the stand." A sixty-year-old, blue-collar, hard-working man is helped to the stand by John, the bailiff, due to his arm and leg wrapped in a cast. He is the picturesque sympathetic victim, with old yet kind eyes and strong, calloused hands. Fit, but with a teddy bear belly. His wallet, no doubt, is filled with pictures of his wife and grandkids. Ready to quick-draw and show off and dote on with little provocation.

"Is that really his name?" Judge Albert asks, looking through his papers.

"I'm sorry to say Witness One doesn't have one. Our defendant felt no need to give one to a 'simple gag character.'" Mr. Stu says, invoking John, the bailiff, to glare daggers at Harry.

Realizing Harry is already in a bad light, he jumped from his seat, "Objection! Improper character evidence! He is using biased language to make the jury prejudiced."

Without missing a beat, as if Mr. Stu precisely knew what Harry would say, Mr. Stu asks, "Oh? Have you given him a name? What was his role? If either, what is his name and role so that the court can properly address him?"

"It's uhh. I uhh…" Harry tries to think of a name to suddenly give Witness One, but it is hard without looking up a random one on the internet. "I withdraw my objection," Harry says, slinking back to his seat as he realizes everyone is staring at him.

"You may proceed." Judge Albert instructs.

Mr. Stu continues, "Thank you. Now, Witness One - I'm sorry, is it alright if I call you that?"

"I'll take whatever name I can call my own." Witness One says in a weak voice.

"Of course. Witness One, could you please tell the jury who you are in relation to the defendant and how you received those injuries?"

Well, I think you put it best, Sonny. I'm just an old, simple, no-named background character. I was born a few years back when Mr. Hawthorn here wrote me in his action novel, "A Soft Kill."

"New York Times best seller!" Harry felt compelled to advertise to the courtroom.

Judge Albert's face is red almost immediately as he shouts, "Unless you have an objection, you will be silent! Continue with your testimony!"

"Right, so, when I was written, the first thing that happened in my life was that I was about to win big at the casino where the scene was taking place. It was apparently my last few days till retirement. The winnings would have given me the break I needed after many years of non-descript blue-collar workman stuff that I suppose I do. My wife and I could have also finally gone on the honeymoon we always dreamt of."

Harry is practically steaming sweat as he knows where this story is going.

"But the protagonist, James Grasper, got into a gunfight with one of the very clearly, but not directly stated, Russian terrorist villains. In the shoot-out, I was written to get hit twice in a bit of tragic ironic humor. I had to spend all my winnings on hospital bills and more. I left with less than I came in. James Grasper was written to say the cheesy one-liner, 'It looks like the house always takes a cut,' After killing the villain."

"Objection!" Harry says again with more confidence this time, "This is hearsay! Per relationem, your honor. There is no way for Witness One to know all this. I didn't write him to break the fourth wall."

Judge Albert sighs, already tired, "You certainly know your legal terms, Mr. Hawthorn."

"Thank you, your honor. I studied them quite a bit for writing my detective and law drama novels. Heck, I'm sure I could pass the BAR with flying colors if I wanted to."

"Regardless." Judge Albert says, ignoring him, "The unknown supernatural forces that brought you here have also given all of us characters self-awareness both now and retroactively. We know how we were created and what went on 'behind the scenes' as it were, in our lives, and at least in respect to the novels we featured in. So the objection is denied."

Mr. Stu gives Harry another devilish grin before saying, "Would you like to cross-examine Witness One's testimony?"

Harry, thinking Mr. Stu is trying to use reverse psychology, takes the bait by saying, "Why yes, I would. Now Mr. Witn-"

"Can I ask you a question, Mr. Hawthorn?" Witness One interrupted.

Harry is fairly certain a witness is not usually allowed to ask questions during cross-examination. His current standing with the witness looks bad enough as is. Letting him ask his question might endear Harry to the jury, or so he thinks. Harry nods and lets him.

"Why did I have to get shot?"

"Oh goddammit." Harry says in his head.

"I didn't harm anyone. You didn't even write me to be grumpy or anything. I had no plot significance," A tear forms in Witness One's eyes as his voice catches, "I wasn't even named!"

Harry's heart races, "Well, I mean, after the heavy scene with James Grasper learning that the Ru-Uh terrorists killed his little brother, I felt that the story needed a little comic relief to lighten the mood."

"Is innocent people getting shot funny to you, Mr. Hawthorn?"

"Of course not! I-I mean-" Harry stammers.

Mr. Stu interrupts, "Witness One, did the defendant at least write the protagonist returning to ensure you and the other civilians were okay?"

"No, after the terrorists were killed and James Grasper saved his one-off girlfriend for that novel, he was written to leave with applause from the police station and go home and get laid. We were just forgotten in the story."

"I-I didn't mean to. It was a plot hole I didn't notice until after publication."

"Thank you, Witness One." Mr. Stu says moving things along, "You may leave now. Your honor, may I call Detective Ben McClintock to the stand?"

"Wait, the hero of my murder mystery trilogy?" Harry asks. "The very same."

Harry makes a sly smile of his own to try and show Mr. Stu how badly he messed up picking Detective McClintock.

Detective McClintock has short, receding, grayish-red hair that he covers with a fedora, broad shoulders, and a suit slightly large for him, probably due to the stress of the job making him eat less and smoke more. As he sits on the bench, he coughs quite a lot and makes everyone in the room feel uncomfortable.

"Detective McClintock, could you please introduce yourself to the court?"

"I'm Detective Ben McClintock of the Chicago police department. It's a rough city that needs rougher cops. I'm from Harry's mystery trilogy, Killer Crimes in Chicago, set in nineteen forty-nine." He says with a voice that only gets so gravelly after smoking since he was eight.

"Thank you. Your honor, if I may, I wish to forgo my direct examination and let Harry begin his cross-examination."

Judge Albert looks perplexed when he asks, "Are you sure?"

"I am."

"Very well. Mr. Hawthorn, you may begin."

Harry doesn't know what Mr. Stu is thinking, but Harry is sure he has this in the bag.

"You saved many lives, correct, Benny?"

"Correct." Detective McClintock says as he pulls out a cigar and continues, " But don't ever call me Benny. You know I hate that."

"Right, sorry, but I also know that it gave you satisfaction to stop those murderers. It was your passion and calling. You enjoyed a good mystery, and I gave you the best. I gave your life adventure and purpose."

"That's true."

Harry smiles as he says, "Nota bene, my dear jur-"

"But that's cold comfort for the victims. Or their friends and families. What do I tell them now? 'Sorry your loved one was horrifically murdered, but they needed to die to give me and the plot purpose.' I'm sure little Susy, whose father you wrote to have been killed by the mob for his gambling debts, would be more than understanding." Detective McClintock says with cold sarcasm.

"Now, hold on! I didn't give everyone a bad ending. You lived through hell and back, and you and your partner Jenny got together at the end of the series after a lot of will-they won't-they." Harry is particularly proud of that one as it was one of his first romance plots.

"That's also true. Jenny was a dame to die for. Some damn fine descriptions you gave her. But it didn't last."

"What? You two broke up? I didn't write that!"

"Our lives don't just end when you finish writing on the page." "Since when?" Harry shouts, terrified and confused about everything going on and all the existential implications being glossed over.

"Objection. Not relevant." Mr. Stu says.

"While I agree, it should be noted that it appears, at the very least, that Mr. Hawthorn is ignorant of our continuation after creation." Judge

Albert remarks.

Detective McClintock ignores Harry's question, not knowing the answer himself, and continues, "I was an old drunk with a bad smoking habit and more character flaws than I can count. Jenny was one of the first female detectives of the era, quick as a whip and tough as nails. She had bright career prospects while I was washed up. And to top it all off, she was half my age. Once I became aware I felt like a sleazebag. Of course, it didn't last, and I don't blame her."

"That's… Surprisingly progressive for you considering the time period you are from."

"What can I say? You wrote me to be a somewhat likable character for modern readers. Though not one that a woman like Jenny could fall for without author interference. Can I go now? I need to see my Oncologist in an hour."

Barely catching himself from stumbling, Harry asks, "Wait! When did you get cancer?"

"Having a smoking and drinking problem doesn't exactly make you the picture of perfect health."

"Thank you, Detective McClintock. You may go now." Mr. Stu says then as he passes Harry on his way to the prosecution table he whispers, "Shall I fetch you more rope for the noose you are tying yourself to?"

"Screw you! You're just a bunch of text with a big mouth written by my moody teen self." Harry whispers back.

Taking the insult in stride Mr. Stu says, "I would like to call in my last witness for today. Your honor, may I call the Dark Lady Supreme, Wielder of the Defiling Dagger, Mistress of the Dark realms, Voldron the Vitriol to the stand."

"What in the goddamn-"

Judge Albert slams his gavel as he shouts, "This is your last warning, Mr. Hawthorn! You will watch your vulgarity while in my courtroom or I shall hold you in contempt. Is that understood?"

"Yes, your honor, but she's a mass murderer! She belongs in prison for all the crimes she committed in my Heroes of the Burning Sunlight young adult fantasy series."

"Only because you wrote me to commit them," Voldron says with a voice that could command legions of undead warriors. She tries to sit on the stand with her large black spiky armor getting in the way. It is hard to see her face as she wears a hood that only shows the oblivion of space to anyone who tries to see her eyes.

"I explicitly wrote that you choose to become evil of your own free will to gain more power for yourself and your dragons."

"You wrote that I chose? Do you not hear the contradiction? If I 'chose' to stay with the benevolent mystic Elves of Lathanalch and become a good wizard of healing, would you have let me?"

"No, that would be boring," Harry says instinctually as if arguing with his editor. He tries to elaborate as he sees the jury looking at him with disgust, "I mean, there wouldn't be a story! There needed to be an inciting action and conflict for readers to be interested. L-look, my stories have inspired millions. I have saved lives with my art and encouraged many to become writers at least half as great as me."

Voldron is silent for a moment. Harry hopes that maybe he is getting somewhere. But then she says, "If having innocent creations, fresh from the womb of the quill or keyboard as you call it, being forced to suffer or do evil acts is required for humans to be inspired, perhaps you were correct to have me desire their destruction."

"That is enough!" Judge Albert says with another slam of his gavel. "You are dismissed."

Harry covers his face with his hands, whispering, "This can't be happening to me. I've made too much beauty in the world to go to prison. Especially by the very characters I wrote."

While Mr. Stu packs his papers in his quality leather briefcase, he can't help but whisper again to Harry, "What are your measurements? We want to make sure your new outfit is slimming. You heard orange is the new black, right?"

In a fit of frustration and more than likely grasping for straws, Harry screeches, "Your honor! I call Prosecutor Stu to the stand!"

"You can't call a Prosecutor to the stand." Judge Albert says, rubbing his temples.

"You also can't hold a trial without the defendant having a public attorney. If you can break the rules so can I. Cessante ratione legis cassat ipsa lex, your honor."

"Very well. I will grant you this concession. Though I fail to see how this will aid your case."

Without a word, Mr. Stu casually strolls to the stand.

"Can you tell the court who you are and where you are from?"

Patronizingly, Mr. Stu says, "As I told the court before. I am Prosecutor Gary Stu. As for where I am from, I am sad to say I was your self-insert for your fan fiction of the legal drama Courting the Courtroom.

"Yes, I will admit you were not my finest work. I was a young teenager still honing my writing perfection. I made you perfect without any character flaws. Great at everything, perfect health, with massive wealth.

Married to the most attractive woman in the series. So why do you hate me?"

With barely a twinge in his lip, Mr. Stu asks, "Excuse me? It would be highly unprofessional and unethical to be your prosecutor if I had such a bias against you."

Suddenly gaining confidence back, Harry continues, "Don't kid yourself. I've learned from my life that if someone hates me, it is solely for a few specific reasons. Either because they see me as a threat, they hate themselves, or they want to be me. Which is it, Gary? Scire facias."

"Have you considered that maybe, they hate you for being a narcissist?" Mr. Stu says thinking that was the end of it.

"Not even once."

"Of course you didn't. You're so full of yourself."

"Incorrect, I can't get enough of myself. I need more of myself. And it seems you are threatened by how close I've come to being like you. Except unlike you, I had to work for it."

Anger becomes visible on Mr. Stu's face, and his voice sounds like a scratching chalkboard as he says, "You don't know what it is like to be 'perfect,' far from it."

"Perfect? Please, you were a first draft at best." Stu's eyes roll at Harry's comment, but Harry continues, "And you call me the narcissist? You act like you are fighting for the characters, but you have profited off my writing more than my publishers. Everyone would be jealous about the life I gave you free of charge."

Mr. Stu nearly lunges at Harry as he shouts like a madman, "Do you think I like being perfect at everything? Can you imagine the boredom of never having to be challenged at anything? The impossibility of making friends when they feel lesser around you? How it damages my marriage because my wife can't stop comparing herself to me and feels like she can never measure up no matter how much I tell her I love her the way she is?"

And with his characteristic smug grin returning, Harry says, "Looks to me we have a clear case of conflict of interest, your honor. A Praeiudicium, as it were. It would be a perversion of Justice if a mistrial is not declared immediately! It is abundantly clear everything Gary has said and all the evidence he has presented is tainted."

Judge Albert takes his time to consider. On the one hand, Harry is correct. The rules of the courtroom have already been bent beyond reason. On the other hand, no court out of the pages would accept this case, and even less likely would they favor fictitious characters over their own. The only way to get a new prosecutor and defense would be to have

Harry write them. And clearly, he would have a conflict of interest now that he is aware.

"Due to the unprecedented and near-impossible circumstances of this case, the only way to maintain fairness and protect the rights of the defendant is to dismiss the case. I cannot judge whether you, Harry, are guilty or innocent while maintaining my integrity. I don't know if anyone in the pages can."

A STAR OF ASH:
A TALE FROM SAIGŌHON

It all happened a few months after the Sanctus Venatores of the Beacon land Bastiel declared the Second Grand Crusade in the year 9,413. Only sixteen years prior, the Bastielians had their petty civil war that devastated their nation. Many of the Daimyo [7]felt the declaration was a foolish demonstration of bravado. Or perhaps ravenous revolutionary fervor at risk of consuming itself if left with no other prey to feast upon. Of course, our own Venatores Sōhei[8] were in favour. Even in my youth, it was clear they chafed as the Onmyo[9] Mages were given positions at court above them. Some did not want to lose our blessed peace while no one assailed us.

The Kami [10]Umba and Gillian had protected our beautiful land from The Era of Despair, or so we thought in our arrogance. However, the decision was up to his Divine Imperial Majesty Aoibara Daichi[11]. Despite protests, he decided to enlist our nation in the cause of the Second Grand Crusade.

'It was our destiny to reshape the world in our image, so that all could enjoy the prosperity we cherish.' Was what Emperor Aoibara proclaimed, according to my honored father, Heishi Makoto[12].

It was that final breath, the last brush stroke of that proclamation, that we had finally learned the debt our 'blessing' accrued. I was too young to

7 Daimyo - A feudal lord/noble. Pronounced Die-m-yo.

8 Sōhei - Pronounced So-hey.

9 Onmyo - Pronounced Awn-m-yo.

10 Kami - Means god(s). Pronounced Kah-mee.

11 Aoibara Daichi - A name. Pronounced Ah-o-ee-ba-ra Die-chee.

12 Heishi Makoto - A name. Pronounced Hey-she Ma-koh-toh.

understand the politics of the time. But old enough to fight in the wars they wrought.

***

It was after my first battle. My toes had burned and bled from the thongs of my sandals. I don't recall how long I had walked, though I believed it was close to the hour of the rooster as the amber sun was blazing the horizon. My armour was once as vibrant as sandy beaches and pure as the clouds. Gifted to me by my father and to him by his father. I had gotten it caked in mud and blood as it shambled and chafed against my broken, red-feathered wings.

Panic should have taken my heart at the prospect of my lost flight. Of never seeing the clouds as my peers and the trees and mountains as my underlings. Even now, I shudder at the memory as I write this. But at the time, all I could think about was finding the Daimyo I served, Lord Raikomo Haruto[13]. I couldn't stop to process the ramifications of my injury. Even if it rains or if spears fall.

I am aware I have been meandering so much when so little has happened in my story, but I'm old now, dammit. I earned my right to ramble!

Returning to my thoughts. I had lost my helmet when I awoke. Which was just as well since my five-inch long, broken nose would have made it impossible to fit. I had not the faintest idea of how much further I needed to travel, yet I knew I needed to reach there before it was too late. How or why I had such knowledge, I can't say. Perhaps it was the will of the Kami, karma, or dumb luck.

A few hours had passed before I found the dirt roads between the rice fields. I had almost collapsed and prayed thanks to the Kami Umba and Gillian, but haste was required of me. I was so close and could finally see it. A sight of such heresy. The Eternal City of Oriso[14] set ablaze.

The smoky sky was painted with crimson and amber wisps by the violent brushes of the castles and temples. I grabbed hold of the swords on my side and ran. I ran as the screaming of peasants and Tanuki[15] merchants grew louder. I ran as black ash began to fall like snow and burning arrows poured like rain. I ran until the air felt like needles in my lungs and forced me to crawl on all fours. I wanted to ignore it all. It was too much chaos, too much inside my head. For those too young or too foreign to understand, witnessing the Eternal City turn to ruin was as

---

[13] Raikomo Haruto - A name. Pronounced Rah-Eye-koh-moh Ha-roo-toe.

[14] Oriso - A name. Pronounced Oh-ree-so.

[15] Tanuki - A mythological creature. Pronounced Tah-nue-key.

unfathomable, as if the Tower of Babel crumbled or the sun blackened. But again, I needed to focus on my duty. I saw an abandoned cart and crawled underneath it. I tried to force my broken wing to fit in, and I accidentally sucked in a lungful of smoke after yelping in pain like a pathetic dog. I rested until I could stop coughing.

"What madness has the Crusade brought to light? Saigōhon[16] was supposed to be better than this. We were supposed to be united. We were supposed to save The Known World!" I childishly thought before crawling back out.

I had not understood how close I was to the Heavenly Aoibara castle until I peered toward the sky. Its snow-white walls had been greyed with ash. Its rose blue shingles had wilted and were crumbling from the heat. I could not see Lord Raikomo in the carnage and slaughter; if he was in the city, he would be in the castle defending Emperor Aoibara. I mused that if I could fly up there and join the defense, perhaps Lord Raikomo would have forgiven me and allowed me to fight alongside him in some sort of heroic last stand. But life would never be that simple.

I tried to skirt around the castle to find the gates. Suddenly, a cumbersome cluster of clothes crashed into me. It was a strange day, looking back. I gazed heavenward and surmised someone from the castle heights was attempting to escape with a very expensive makeshift rope.

If it had been Emperor Aoibara or his heir, perhaps I could scramble my way up there and attempt to save them, was what I had thought.

"A Tengu[17], climbing like an animal! Such disgraceful behaviour!" I knew my father would have shouted had he learned what I did.

I had wrapped my hands around the rope and pulled myself upward. With each pull, the muscles in my arms came closer to how my legs felt. As I saw the ledge coming closer, I convinced my body to go on a little bit further. When I had only five feet left, I heard shouting up above.

"Please, I beg you to stay here!" An older woman's voice pleaded. Her dingy servant's clothes brushed around the ledge like a broom.

"Perhaps a handmaiden to the heir?" I thought as my hands finally reached the wooden guard rails of the balcony. I pulled myself over and fell to my knees, breathing heavily and thankful that the smoke was lighter up here. How humans and Yokai [18]- Sorry, Demi -Humans, of similar shapes, use only their hands and feet for travel. I will never comprehend.

"My Lady, getaway!" Screamed the older handmaiden. I finally saw

---

[16] Saigōhon - A name. Pronounced Sigh-go-hawn.

[17] Tengu - A mythological creature. Pronounced Ten-goo.

[18] Yokai - A classification of mythological creatures. Pronounced Yo-Kah-Eye.

who she was talking to. It wasn't the heir of Aoibara, nor was it the Emperor himself.

It was a woman. Her long, waxed-shine, brown hair looped in the back and was held together by a silver and sapphire jeweled comb. Her powdered, porcelain white, oshiroi[19] makeup covered her entire face, allowing her short nose and slightly squarish jaw to express herself beyond doubt.

She wore a Yukata[20] as white as fresh snow on the mountains of home with deep, ocean-blue rose petals dancing around her slender body. What more could I say to truly show you her splendor and mature grace, especially for a human. I was stunned by her beauty... As well as by the shaft of her Naginata[21] as it slammed into my head.

It took me a moment to recall the world and my place in it, then I shouted with my youthful cracking voice, "Wait! I'm here to help! I'm with the Raikomo!" Before she could slash the bladed end of her weapon at my neck.

"The Raikomo? Has your Clan finally arrived? Have you brought reinforcements?" The woman asked in a voice as pleasant as a shamisen[22] played masterfully.

"Arrived? Is he not here already?" I had asked, while feeling the pangs of terror creep in.

She turned away from me and told her handmaiden, "We need to leave, now."

"We can't use your rope. No doubt someone saw this Tengu boy climbing up here." The old human handmaiden hissed as she scowled at me as though I were a delinquent child caught running away. I would have taken offense, but my mind was uselessly racing for any possible explanation for Lord Raikomo's absence that was not the truth.

The woman turned back to me, and a sly thought seemed to cross her mind. She lowered herself to look me in the eyes and said, "I am Aoibara Yoshino[23], daughter of the Divine Emperor Aoibara. Please introduce yourself."

As soon as her name had registered in my mind, all of my previous thoughts were dashed. I immediately prostrated before her. "I am Heishi

---

19 Oshiroi - Pronounced Oh-she-roy.
20 Yukata - A light long robe. Pronounced You-kah-tah.
21 Naginata - A bladed pole-arm. Pronounced Nah-ghee-nah-tah.
22 Shamisen - A string instrument. Pronounced Sha-mee-sen.
23 Yoshino - A name. Pronounced Yo-she-no.

Jun[24] of Injō [25]province, Samurai to Lord Raikomo. Please forgive my poor manners and appearance, Lady Aoibara. Both were forgotten in all of the chaos."

Lady Aoibara smiled in a way that was both reassuring and surreptitious, "There is no need for forgiveness for your circumstance is understood. I do request your help though."

The handmaiden interrupted her and said, "My lady, look at him, the boy can't fly anymore and he looks like he'll collapse any minute."

Lady Aoibara looked back at her with scorn and said, "I don't care. I refuse to be the Koregomo's[26] plaything. Do not try to stop me."

"I can do it," I offered without a thought in my head. Desperate to preoccupy myself from my wings and the fate of Lord Raikomo. Escorting such a breathtaking royal was certainly a pleasant distraction in my opinion.

She smiled again, a sight I could never have my fill of, "Perfect! Then follow me. Our only means of escape we have left is through a secret passage in the castle. However, it is on the lower floor. No doubt the Koregomo brutes are already trying to reach us up here. If you can protect us, I will be able to find the passage. It will take us far into the rice fields outside the castle."

"A wise plan! We should hurry." I said as I heard the screeches of the Koregomo warcry marching closer.

"Of course, let me just-" Lady Aoibara stopped short before handing the naginata to the handmaiden and grabbed a small oddly plain looking lockbox. "Lead the way."

I kept my hand on my sword as we walked through the castle halls and headed toward the stairs. One of the Koregomo Ashigaru[27] rushed up toward us. The Ashigaru, like most of the clan she served, was a silver-furred, red-faced, Satori[28] of the snowy Hirasumi[29] Mountains. She wore little armour aside from a simple black cuirass. Allowing her to climb more easily like her monkey kin.

She probably knew where we were by listening to our thoughts. She let out a screech before striking with her spear, not realising that the castle's small corridors made her long weapon impractical; the back end

---

24 Jun - A name. Pronounced June.

25 Injō - A name. Pronounced Een-joe.

26 Koregomo - A name. Pronounced Koh-ray-go-moh.

27 Ashigaru – Peasant infantry foot soldier. Pronounced Ah-she-gah-roo.

28 Satori - A mythological creature. Pronounced Sah-toe-ree.

29 Hirasumi - A name. Pronounced He-rah-sue-mee.

bounced against the wall behind her. My hand instinctively ripped my katana from the saya [30] and cleanly cut through her neck. Just as my father had taught me. That was the second time in my life I had killed someone.

The first time was in a duel when I was sixteen. It was against a low-born Kappa[31] Samurai of the small Otatsuki[32] Clan to the south. His name was Faiyahanma Shiro[33], and he felt my father didn't give his Lord proper reverence. Which, for such a minuscule vassal to the Ishido[34], did not warrant much consideration, in my opinion, with Faiyahanma himself being the exception.

My father saw this as the perfect opportunity to demonstrate to our Daimyo, Lord Raikomo, the results of his tutelage.

I was enthralled by how proper and ceremonial it was. My opponent was respectful and gracious. Allowing me to set the conditions of the duel, as I was only half his age at the time. Forgoing his great advantage in the rivers. Everything was so organised and fair. Nothing like the horrendous chaos of total warfare. His death was well-fought and dignified.

The same could not be said of the Ashigaru. Her body fell down the steps with what would have been comical thudding and rolling if there weren't more of them in the castle. If the other Satori weren't paying attention to our thoughts, that noise would have alerted them.

"Run!" I shouted. Our only hope was to rush them without giving them a chance to coordinate. We reached the lower level and what appeared to be the servants' quarters. We saw a mix of Yokai and Oni[35] thieves, most likely Yakuza[36] due to their body tattoos, Rōnin[37] bandits, and Ashigaru looting from the castle. They howled and charged at me, and I tried to block the first one with my sword, but the second went to my left, and the third climbed the ceiling to go after Lady Aoibara. I've always hated fighting indoors. Not enough room to fly and fighting two-dimensionally is infuriating, to say the least.

Fortune had shown me favour for the moment, as a bellowing roar came from the other end of the room, "STAND DOWN!"

---

30 Saya - A scabbard. Pronounced Sah-yah.
31 Kappa - A mythological creature. Pronounced Kah-pah.
32 Otatsuki - A name. Pronounced Oh-taht-sue-kee.
33 Faiyahanma Shiro - A name. Pronounced Fie-ya-hann-ma She-row.
34 Ishido - A name. Pronounced Ee-she-dough.
35 Oni - A classification of mythological creatures. Pronounced Oh-knee.
36 Yakuza - A group of organized criminals. Pronounced Ya-coo-za.
37 Rōnin - A masterless Samurai. Pronounced Row-neen.

The voice was so deep as to make my stomach quake, and his allies backed away. The Satori Samurai was a giant of his kind. He had to duck to get through the sliding door. He had an intricate obsidian kabuto[38] with a blood-red men-yoroi [39]and a silver-haired mustache attached. The enraged expression on the mask was almost enough to obscure his puffy mouth but not enough to hide his jubilance. His armour was of similar colour and bore the symbol of the Koregomo clan. A red arrow piercing storm clouds like a fool trying to attack the Heavens. It was clear to even an idiot such as myself that he was a Samurai of prowess and high rank.

"None of these pompous-pampered Lords are worth the blood and shit that now stains the floors. What about you, boy? You look like you've at least used your sword before." The Giant said as he pulled out his Ōdachi.[40] The curved sword would be considered huge to a normal-sized man, but to him, it was to scale.

"You need to go now, Lady Aoibara." The old handmaiden said as she stood next to me with the naginata. Lady Aoibara obeyed and headed to a nearby wall where she felt her hand around the wood. I wondered what she was doing, but my thoughts were interrupted as the giant charged toward us and swung his massive sword.

"Focus on the fight, dammit!" The Giant shouted as his sword came crashing towards me. Had he not warned me, there was a good chance I would have been cut in half. I had been able to block it by placing my left hand against the blunt of my sword and was knocked over. I somehow managed to land on top of my broken wing and had the wind knocked out of me.

"Not bad, boy." The giant said as he picked me up to my feet and pushed me back. "But keep your back foot balanced and twist with the impact." He continued as if instructing a dojo. He was about to strike at me again, perhaps hoping I picked up the quick lesson, but the old handmaiden tried to chop him.

The giant grabbed the shaft with one hand and said, "This fight is between honest warriors. Not scheming court pets." Before throwing it and the old handmaiden holding it against the wooden pillar. I heard a crack, but it wasn't from the Naginata. Her frail body went limp.

I heard a click near where Lady Aoibara was. I turned and saw that the wall was hiding a tunnel. Lady Aoibara was inside and was about to tell me to follow. But she saw the handmaiden's body. Lady Aoibara was

---

[38]Kabuto - Samurai helmet. Pronounced Kah-boo-toe.

39 Men-yoroi - Samurai war mask. Pronounced Men-yo-roy.

40 Ōdachi - Heavy two-handed sword. Pronounced Oh-da-chee.

too terrified to speak. I pulled myself back to my feet and tried to breathe, but my lungs failed. The Satori Samurai slashed again and again. Each attempt at parrying felt like thunder in my palms, and I nearly lost my grip.

"You're wielding a sword, not strangling a peasant! Loosen the grip, or I'll loosen your hands from your arms." He shouted at me, his spit spraying my face.

I had let my ego get the better of me, and I kicked him in the stomach with a solid thud. He barely flinched and let out an ironically high screeching laugh.

"Excellent. Don't think, act, but know your enemy's weakness next time you leave yourself open!" He said as he slammed his head into mine to emphasise the point. The attack knocked me over to the tunnel. All I could see were stars, but I rolled with the momentum to get inside. Yoshino pulled the lever, releasing a heavy slab of metal in front of the entrance. Preventing the Giant and his allies from following us.

My injuries had finally caught up with me. I had no more adrenaline to keep me awake. I passed out. I did not know how much time had passed. When I woke, I had Lady Aoibara's small lock box on my lap. I felt myself being dragged through the stony tunnel by my armour's openings. When I saw it was Lady Aoibara, I was surprised by her strength. Though now I know the reason for it.

"Are you alright?" I asked her and she ever so gently let me go.

"Yes... Thank you."

I remember trying to stand again, but my legs were collapsing from under me.

"You need to lie down,"

"I must not. If they catch us-"

"Then you will be useless since you can't even stand. Now, do as I say, like a good Samurai." Lady Aoibara scolded in a way unlike her royal station. I would be lying if I said her status and the truth of her words were the only reason I obeyed. I laid on my side to let my body get the rest it craved.

There was only a dim light in the dark tunnel. It came from a lantern Lady Aoibara must have found hanging on the walls. The most we could look at was each other. Lady Aoibara inspected me as if browsing through a Tanuki market. Her eyes glowed in the lantern flame. I didn't know humans had that ability, but many creatures do, I suppose.

"Where are you injured?" She asked, though whether out of concern for my well-being or hers, I couldn't say.

I had to take a minute to identify which part of my body wasn't hurt.

"I'm sore all over, but the more distracting injuries are the broken nose, cracked ribs, and the…" I hesitated, and it was quiet. No matter how hard I tried, I couldn't ignore my broken wings. I was a cripple.

Among the Tengu, I was no better than an armless swordsman. I used to believe honourable death was preferable.

***

The Koregomo's stance regarding the Second Grand Crusade was unique. Rather than debating whether Saigōhon should join the war or abstain, they wanted to fight against the Divine Militia. Their position was abundantly clear. Satori don't hold flowers when speaking as they are notorious for their hatred of the subtleties in politics. Which I find to be understandable, if not admirable. If one can read a politician's thoughts and know every promise was a lie, how could one not get frustrated and demand brutal honesty instead? From what my father told me, this made them infuriating to face court. Too many assume their honesty makes them infallible, but belief does not equate to truth.

After the Emperor's decision was made public, the Lord Koregomo gave himself the title Shōgun[41] and demanded for Emperor Aoibara to relinquish all military command to him. The Emperor and the loyal Daimyo, including my Lord Raikomo, thought they could stamp out this rebellion in one fell swoop. We knew that the Koregomo were preparing to attack The Eternal City of Oriso, so our Clan, being directly connected to Aoibara and Koregomo by land and thus the fastest to respond, was sent to march on their territory. Forcing Koregomo's presumedly small army to split into even smaller forces on two fronts. They underestimated their cunning and failed to realize how many people rallied to the Koregomo banner.

Our forces stopped by the Mizu no Michi[42] River to rest for the night before. The Koregomo hid in the trees directly above us, as silent as a mouse. By listening to our thoughts, they knew precisely where we made camp. Which officers to strike first to create the most havoc. Who was keeping watch, and where they patrolled.

They struck at night when we slept and dropped down on us where we were most vulnerable while the Yakuza families supported them to outnumber us. As flyers, we Tengu are masters of the skies. But that night, the trees were their domain.

Bodies on both sides were crashing around me. I couldn't breathe. I thought I was going to drown in all the blood! Nothing was right.

41 Shōgun - Commander in Chief. Pronounced Show-gun
42 Mizu no Michi - A name. Pronounced Me-zoo no Me-chee.

Nothing was how it should be. This wasn't the glorious and honourable war I was promised. It was a slaughter. I couldn't see. All I heard was screaming, screeching, stabbing, and slashing! A cavalry charge came. My mind and body froze. I suspect I was trampled. When I awoke, I was alone, buried under the piled bodies, and had to dig my way out before I made my long walk to Oriso.

***

"How old are you?" Lady Aoibara asked. I thought the question was so bizarre that it made me turn away from my thoughts. She had probably noticed I was breathing heavily.

"I'm twenty-eight," I said with more bravado than I had confidence.

She raised one of her curved eyebrows and said, "Do you want to try that again?"

I gave in immediately and told her the truth, "Eighteen."

"That makes sense. I always preferred younger men."

I felt my face redden. To a non-Tengu, I imagine that would be pretty hard to notice. It didn't help when Lady Aoibara started to caress her fingers up and down my back. For a moment, I thought I had fallen asleep and was dreaming. The daughter of the Emperor, perhaps the only living heir of her Clan, falling for me? It was preposterous. Absolutely scandalous. Especially if the public knew the truth of what eventually happened. My father would have sold every one of our possessions, even our ancestral lands, for a dowry if such an arrangement was even considered for a single thought.

I was about to stop her when her fingers reached one of my wings. But I noticed a faint orangish-yellow ring light up beneath her. Then, a slow-flowing crimson ring was stacked on top of that. Followed by a solid glowing pale-white ring stacked on top of them all. I could feel the bones in my wings move on their own. Yet I didn't feel any pain. It was unnerving yet fascinating.

"After rain falls, the ground hardens." She quietly droned. Perhaps quoting someone.

"I had no idea the Imperial family had an Onmyo," I said, sitting upward and moving the muscles in my wings. It hurt to do so, but the elation of having my wings back was a good anesthetic.

"No one does. We would prefer to keep it that way until we can better understand where our Venatores' allies stand on Magic. Right now they seem unsure, themselves." Lady Aoibara said. Then she sat in front of me and placed her hand on my face.

"W-what kind of Magic is that?" I bubbled out. I wouldn't have even known what it all meant if she had told me, but it was the only thing I could think of to say. "Micro pulses of Electromancy to intercept the pain, Hemomancy to clear out clots and reduce swelling, and Ostómancy to move, set, and fuse the bone back together." Indeed I had no idea what any of that meant and still don't. But I can certainly attest to their results.

"How many do you know?" I asked her.

"Those three are my specialty, but I have mastered sixteen different types." She told me, not paying attention as she used the same Magic again to fix my nose. From what I know of the human Onmyo who protect the shrines, the most skilled and aged among them could only master four or five within their lifetimes.

I tried to ask, "How did you learn-?"

But she interrupted me by saying, "I'm surprised your kind don't have their noses broken all the time considering it's almost a foot from your face."

"Our kind typically does not let others strike our faces."

"So you, in particular, let them smash it. I have to say that it is a unique martial style."

I was outmatched. I bumbled for something witty to say, which I have no doubt would only lead me to further embarrassment, but my mind kept pulling back to my dreaded question.

My worries must have been visible on my face. Yoshino put her hand on my hairless chin and tilted it toward her. I know now she was trying to keep me from panicking by making me focus on her. A nervous, indecisive Samurai would be useless to her. But if Lord Raikomo had died then, that would have made me...

"What happened to Lord Raikomo?" I stupidly blurted out and promptly nipped any moment that might have blossomed.

She sighed and said, "I do not know. Lord Raikomo sent us a message saying he would come to our aid before the Koregomo attacked us. You are the only one from your Clan that arrived. How did you get separated?"

I explained what happened and my assumption of being separated after the battle. She looked past me contemplatively.

"Are you alright?" She asked as she picked up the small lockbox.

I stood, "Yes, thank you, Yoshino," and I curse myself to this day for my lapse in judgement. Had circumstances been different, my family and Clan would have suffered the consequences of my idiocy.

Her ears perked. She turned toward me, eyebrow raised mischievously and a half-suppressed smile close to bursting with laughter, "Yoshino? So bold of you to be this informal with the daughter of the Emperor.

Tisk tisk. Perhaps when this is all over, I shall have you locked away in a private dungeon. Eh, Jun?" She said in mock seriousness.

I almost forgot to breathe, and Yoshino walked out of the tunnel, barely holding back a chuckle.

It took us ten minutes before we reached the end of the tunnel. The first rays of morning's light poured in like a gentle river. The cool, dewy air was like a greeting from an old friend to my throat and lungs. We stepped outside and saw the sun just about to rise from behind the far mountains... And a black-armored giant charging towards us on horseback through the rice fields.

I drew my sword and told Yoshino to hide in the nearby peasant shack. The horse's gallop thundered across the field, splashing up the rice paddies. I got into a defensive stance, preparing to cut through the horse's legs, but it suddenly jolted before it reached me. The chestnut horse was covered in black leather and adorned with the heads of Daimyo Lords and Generals. My Lord Raikomo and his only heir were among them. I had become masterless. A rōnin.

"Here, I was bored out of my skull trying to make a hunt out of the stragglers, and here you are. The Kami must smile upon us." The Giant said, slapping his knee.

"Here I am," I said, keeping my sword out but lowering it for conversation.

"I'm glad to see you. Believe it or not. Haven't had that much fun in a long time. You show promise. A few more years and scars and who knows..."

The Giant patted his horse and announced, "I, General of the Koregomo Shōgunate, Sanjura Goraincho[43], challenge you!"

Before I could look back, he continued, "You don't need to worry about 'Lady Aoibara' she's just a well-placed puppet of the Sanctus Venatores."

"What do you mean?"

"Nothing gets past us, boy. I'll admit it was a clever plan by the Venatores, but you all underestimate us. We were suspicious for a while, but once the Second Grand Crusade began, we knew something was wrong with the Imperial family. Something had changed and they've been awfully agreeable with the Divine Militia and their antics."

"Well, what if I agree with the Divine Militia too?"

"I know you're smart enough not to have an opinion yet. But for the sake of argument, you would be an idiot who's going to let 'Lady Aoibara'

43 Sanjura Goraincho - A name. Pronounced Sahn-jew-rah Go-rah-eye-choh.

sell out Saigōhon to the fanatics of Bastiel."

"You fumbling flea ridden fools!" Yoshino shouted, "You talk about tomorrow, while the mice in the ceiling laugh! You think you can just fight the entire Known World yourself?"

"It's a fight worth having. Whether we live or die, the Known World must remember and fear what we can do whenever they try to enslave us!" General Goraincho said matter of fact.

"You'll kill us all to be a footnote." I caught Yoshino whispering.

"What do you plan to do with Yo…-Lady Aoibara?" I asked, interrupting their pointless politics.

General Goraincho gave me a stern look while scratching his furry chin, "Poor boy, she's already sunk her fangs into you, hasn't she? Don't need to read your mind to see that."

"What will you do to her?" I shouted and am ashamed to say he had successfully provoked me. Another one of their favourite tactics.

"Keep your mind at ease, boy. His Excellency Shōgunate Koregomo wants her alive. At the moment anyway."

Shōgunate, a brutal title. A fitting title.

"And what will you do after?" I asked.

"If you accept my duel and die, I'll try to have her spared as respect to you. Perhaps as a comfortable hostage until all this Second 'Grand Crusade' nonsense is over. If it is ever over."

"Don't Jun! Your wings are healed, you can fly us away." Yoshino warned as she grabbed my arm.

"But he's alone. He is the only one that knows you are still alive. If we flee he will only track us down."

"He's lying to trap you! And besides he is a General, not some poor farmer with a cheap spear, he knows he can kill you."

I don't have the gift of reading people's thoughts as the Satori, but something inside me knew he was being honest to some extent.

"Why does someone of your rank wish to duel me?"

"Why? Why! Didn't your father ever boast to you? The Tengu of the Raikomo clan are legendary! They gifted us many of the Sword Saints. How can anyone who calls themselves a warrior not yearn for that enlightenment?"

I had judged General Goraincho prematurely. Despite his brutish nature, he did not crave bloodshed, but instead, sought wisdom that could only be obtained from conflict. This was how a fight between Samurai should be.

"I, Jun Heishi of the Raikomo Clan, gladly accept."

General Goraincho smiled widely and drew his massive sword. He held the hilt of his blade parallel to his face with the guard just slightly above his brow. I had positioned my sword in front of me in the middle stance. Ready to attack or defend as needed. We stood, waiting for each other to make the first strike. Several heartbeats passed. Morning dew slid down the edge of my katana and fell when it reached the tip. When it finally splashed on the grass, General Goraincho charged.

General Goraincho swung his sword diagonally, shouting, "EI!" As he tried to cleanly cut my neck. I raised my sword to meet his in a swift motion and guided his blade under mine and turned it safely away from me.

"Good! Finally got the hang of it." He said and I tried to use this opening to stab straight at his chest, but either he was quick enough or knew what I was thinking and jumped back just out of my reach.

"Don't think! Act!" He shouted again.

I tried to go around him and get his left, but he backhanded me and nearly knocked me unconscious.

"I know I said don't think, but don't act stupid."

It's difficult to fight a skilled warrior who knows what you think. Only those who mastered Mujushin[44], the Sword of No Abiding Mind, could perfectly counter them. As you probably have noticed, in all my ramblings and tangents, keeping my mind clear is a challenge for me.

He swung again. This time horizontally, as if he was going to fell a tree. I ducked at the last second. Out of sheer instinct, I flapped my wings. My back burned like having hot coals placed on my skin. But I was already ten feet in the air. I tried to do a swoop slash as my father taught me and had me repeat over a thousand times in practice. I had hoped that my body would follow instinct without thought.

But I guess my memory of the lesson was projected into General Goraincho's mind. He was already in the perfect counter stance. Arms raised and feet ready to spring. I didn't have enough time to change course, and had I kept going, he would have split my skull. Suddenly, the pain in my back prevented me from flapping my wings again. I crashed into the ground, sliding across the dewy grass. I had somehow managed to skid right behind him.

I panicked from the unexpected fall and chopped deep into his calf. I crawled back up before he could fall or retaliate. General Goraincho crouched to try and stop the bleeding with one of his hands. I charged him to take advantage of his lack of mobility. General Goraincho had tried to raise his other hand above his head to have his sword chop down

---

44 Mujushin - A sword technique. Pronounced Moo-jew-sheen.

at me. He had known before I could move that I was about to charge. Yet his pain and having only one hand on his heavy sword slowed him down just enough for me to stab him through his armpit before he could bring his blade down.

I kept my Katana in there for three heartbeats until he finally dropped his sword. I pulled mine out as quickly as I could. Trying to avoid any unnecessary pain. His hot blood splattered on the grass, releasing steam. With a practiced flourish, I swiped my blade in the air and slid the sword back into my saya. It was a foolish attempt at performance. A terrible way to try and clean your Katana! I had to spend many hours re-polishing the damn sword and getting the dried blood out.

"A little sloppy, but well done." General Goraincho chuckled. "How old are you, boy?"

"Eighteen." I would not even attempt to lie to him. He was honest, honorable, and dying.

"Hah! Ha ha ha ha! Fantastic. Fantastic! Killed by… By a boy? I think… I would be proud… If my bastard daughter had your skill… Might even… Let her take my name."

"Why not pray for her to have your strength?"

"No… I don't think… My size is natural… Even among Satori… It may give me incredible strength, I'm not that old, yet… My joints ache… And my heart… If I didn't die today I would have died in my bed… No way… for a Samurai to die… Disgraceful…" He spat blood on the ground defiantly.

"Can you honour my last request?"

"Of course." I told him.

"Grab the gourd off my horse."

I ran and grabbed the gourd and opened it. It had a fruity smell of strong sake. I gave the gourd to his good arm, and he took two gulps.

"Do you… know how to do this… boy?" General Goraincho asked.

"I've only seen it done." By Daimyo, Lord Raikomo's eldest son, Kaito. I only discovered the true reason later. He and his friends got drunk and tortured peasants for amusement. The cover up was just a small coin in the crippling debt our blessed peace cost.

"With your skill, I think that will be good enough." General Goraincho unstrapped his cuirass and moved the folds of his kimono[45] to reveal his furry stomach. He handed me a fold of paper, and I drew his wakizashi [46]for him and handed it to him. He aimed the point of the

---

45 Kimono - A type of dress robe. Pronounced Key-moe-no.
46 Wakizashi - A short sword. Pronounced Wah-key-zah-she.

blade toward himself, and I drew my katana, stood ready, and gave him a nod.

General Goraincho plunged the wakizashi into his stomach and dragged it from his left to his right. He was silent and strong as the mountains. When he was finished he exhaled and nodded. I brought my sword down and removed his head before he could make a sound.

Yoshino came out of hiding when it was finished, "What does it say?" She asked.

I opened the paper, "Drink deeply from life. Death is satiated for now. May my blood flow strong." and I have committed it to memory.

"What will you do now?" I asked Yoshino.

She held the lockbox close to her chest and said, "If the Divine Militia are still our ally, I hope that I can use this to get their protection."

"What is it?" I asked her.

She was hesitant at first, but she said, "Some of my family's gold and other valuable trinkets. Enough to pique the interest of even the higher Daimyo."

"You will want to hide that. Who knows what many people would do to get that kind of fortune." With that wealth I could have made myself a vassal.

"Where will you go?" Yoshino had asked me.

"With my Lord's death and my duty failed, the only way to keep my family from dishonour is to find someone who will do for me what I have done for General Goraincho."

"Or you can come with me?" Yoshino had suggested and looked as though she were holding her breath. I looked deep into her eyes. So full of wisdom, charm, and cunning. For a brief moment, I thought I saw two or three tails behind her. I blinked, and they were gone.

A STAR OF ASH:
THEIR FIRST SOULS OF SAINTS DAY
(SPOILERS FOR A CHILD OF MAGIC)

If you lived in the Port Town Valour in Bastiel, the evening sun would set parallel to the cloud-breaking Tower of Babel on the horizon. 'A gift of life and love from Gillian and a gift of structure and society from Umba,' Ava had once told Kal sometime before she disappeared. Ava loved sharing stories about her homeland, while Kal simply loved listening to her. Watching her teal hair flow past her grassy green eyes, how her chest heaved in the brief moments she paused, and when her heart-shaped lips smiled at a friend.

He had difficulty imagining the many wonders she tried to convey, from the undeniably colossal Tower of Babel to the subtle emerald green hills and the crystal blue rivers that feed into the vast ocean.

"The snow falls early this year? Eh, vennen lille min," Kal mused while keeping the hands warm of Ava's little gift within his own gloved hands. This winter wasn't as bitter and unforgiving as Kal and his newborn Freya's first. That year was an extreme experience that he would die happy to never repeat. Kal spent all the gold he had from the Second Grand Crusade to reach Bastiel, so their only shelter from the cold was his traveling tent in the nearby forest and whatever campfire he could make.

Those desperate days of keeping Freya warm and safe from wild animals and monsters felt almost like a far-off fever dream, as this year, Kal was finally able to save enough money from selling potions to buy an old storage shack on a hill just outside of town. Kal had never had a house before, as far as he could remember, but he knew from their first night inside it was vastly superior to any tent or fort he slept in. He couldn't even begin to imagine what it was like for those people with long titles who lived in bigger houses. Kal didn't know what to do with all the space his two-room shack had now.

"Pappa! Pappa! Pappa!" Little Freya squeaked with sheer delight as she bounced on his lap and pointed at the excited crowds. Freya just turned four last spring and had already started school this fall. She was already looking so much like Ava, but his dusty brown eyes sparkled back at Kal whenever Freya looked at him. Kal would be overjoyed if his Freya grew to have even half her mother's goodness.

"A hundred hearts would be too few for you two." Kal thought as he kissed the top of Freya's head.

From his hilltop view, Kal could see the gathering people setting up streamers, stands, stalls, and snacks. If Kal understood the customs correctly, today was Souls of Saints Day. As Ava had explained, at the end of fall, right after harvest, Bastiellians would remember and celebrate people called Saints. Who, as Kal understood, was considered someone of great importance even long after death. She tried to teach him the traditions and their meaning in the Fidelium faith, but try as he might, Kal couldn't wrap his head around it. In his mind, the only important ones were Ava and their daughter, Freya.

But even in the darkest days of the Second Grand Crusade, Ava had tried to get their camp to celebrate. In the few years Kal had lived in Valour, he hadn't partaken in the Souls of Saints Day festival. Of course, on the one hand, Kal was too focused on everything needed to make sure Freya was safe and fed. On the other hand, he was uncomfortable with all the noise and crowds.

"Do you want to go there, vennen lille min?" Freya nodded her little head like a woodpecker.

"This day meant much to your mother. Perhaps it would be good for us to know and be known by the locals," Kal whispered to Freya, probably too young to understand all he said, but was happy anyway. Kal barely knew how to get to the schoolhouse since he walked Freya there with the Conalls for the past few months. Without them, he would have been hopelessly lost. Kal dusted the snow that collected on his big black pointed hat, wrapped Freya around his back with an old scarf, and headed down their hill toward the town. Freya cheered the whole way down.

***

"Need a place to rest for a night of celebration? Come by our Starboard Tavern and Inn! We keep the food hot, the drinks cold, and the beds warm!" A young woman shouted on the streets. She wore a white mask of a Saint Kal did not know. Not that he knew many, to begin with. Apparently the masks are meant so people could do good deeds in secret, but Kal found the masks disturbing.

As for the Starboard Inn, Kal had been there only one time before. It was when Freya was ill from the cold and couldn't survive another night in their tent. He had to sell his old spear the Divine Militia armed him with to afford it.

"Heey, kid! Doon't suuppoose yoouu knoow if the Baath Hoouuse heeree caateers to Deemi-Huumaans liikee me doo yaa?" An old grey-haired Korrigan[47] crowned in autumn flowers whispered to Kal. Nearly yanking him to the ground with a tug on his sleeve. That way, the short Korrigan could reach Kal's ear.

Kal didn't know, not able to afford to see for himself. He tried to pull away. But even at the Korrigan's old age, his effortless grip could crush stone. Kal had no way to force himself away without using Magic which would be... Problematic in the middle of town. Freya giggled at the silly spectacle.

"Why are you dancing, Pappa?"

"Your Da's just happy to meet an old friend of ours."

"Daanaa! Hoows the craaic?" The old Korrigan asked Missus Dana Conall.

"Craic's been mighty! Glad to see you again, old hairy face. Mind letting go of Kal before he drops his precious cargo?" Missus Conall asked, wearing her leather armour that matched the colour of her hair from her time as a mercenary. It took a second and a few squints for the old Korrigan to understand her meaning. He released Kal's sleeve once he saw Freya on his back.

"Soorry aboouut thaat, Laad." The Korrigan said, dusting off Kal's jacket. "Yoouu geet distraacteed eeaasily in my aagee." He looked Kal up and down a few times, "Goods aboove, yoouu're ah spitting paainting of my Graandsoon, maay hee reest in peeacee. Thee waar toook him tooo sooon."

"You're as blind as an Aos Sí above ground! Kal has nary a hair on his chin." Missus Conall laughed.

"Ooh, sood ooff yoouu, yoouungsters!" The Korrigan shouted, waving his fist around. Kal instinctively thought of spell formulations before the old Korrigan started walking away, "I'll seee yoouu and Toom laateer for ah pint, Daanaa."

"You too, Hairy Face!" Missus Conall said, waving to him while Freya

47 Korrigan - A mythological creature. Pronounced Core-ree-gan.

did the same. Kal noticed the arming sword on her waist.

"Is there trouble?" Kal asked.

"Nope, and I'm going to keep it that way. Can't trust the Dock Guards not to enjoy the festivities a little too much. I'll be taking Brigid out too once she finishes cleaning herself up. My turn this year while Tommy gets to stay home and sell stuff for the festival. Is this your first Souls of Saints day or did they have them where you were from?"

Kal didn't know where he was from and didn't allow himself to think about it. He nodded, not sure what else to say.

"Well it's bout time you took the little tyke down here," Missus Conall said as she ruffled Freya's long teal hair.

"How's she been? Adjusting to your new place well?"

"Ja… Takks again for feeding her I-"

"Not another word about it, Kal. Only the cruel let children starve. As a proper gal of Gillian, I'm more than happy to help."

Kal felt he ought to thank her again but realised that would go against what she just told him. Not sure how to handle his dilemma, he chose silence.

After a while, it became awkward until Missus Conall broke the silence, "I hope I'm not opening old wounds, but I know eyes that've seen horror. My company and I saw plenty of it." Kal's breath catched, but he didn't know why. "I don't know what you've been through, but I know that you're awfully young to be a father and too young to have those kinds of eyes. Are you sure you can handle this? The Orphan City of Charity can take care of Freya for you."

"She will not be taken from me!" Kal rasped, more harshly than he wanted.

Without a flinch, Missus Conall said, "Sorry. It wasn't my place to say. If you ever want to talk, our house is always open to you two. But for now why don't you two enjoy the festival. Don't let me keep you."

That was obvious enough of a queue that even Kal could understand. He nodded and made his way. Kal regretted this being the last conversation they had. Missus Conall would die of sickness a couple years later. Kal would visit Mister Conall every now and then out of respect for them both.

Kal reached the center of town where 'historical' plays of the Saints were performed. Although he didn't know the actual events, Kal learned plenty from his time in the Crusade that Bastiel tended to alter facts for their benefit.

The violet stage curtains were violently pulled back and out came a woman in tatters with her skin painted bluish-green like a drowned corpse. Puppets designed to look like snakes dangled from a string all around her. She made a weird hissing noise and Freya hid her face behind Kal's shoulder.

"Fear? What, pray thee, is there to fear? By the benevolence of the Gods, fear is but a void where faith hath not yet found its abode. Shouldst thou brim thine heart with faith, fear shall find no dwelling, and it shall ebb away, engulfing demons and heathens in its wake." A man in emerald green robes said as he slowly walked onto the stage. He held a clover in one hand and a large, gold painted goblet in the other and wore a porcelain mask of a man with long hair and an even longer beard. If Kal remembered correctly, Ava told him this was Bastiel's most venerated Saint Patrick. The lifeless masks set Kal the wrong way.

"Though chains be absent, thy servitude shall endure eternal!" The woman hissed dramatically.

"Thou art mistaken, foolish dope!" They paused waiting for the children to finish laughing.

"Those who safeguard Gillian's children, and with unwavering devotion and obedience, heed each utterance of Umba, they are truly free. With these waters I banish thee and thy serpents away from Bastiel forever!" And the man in green robes forced the woman's head into the goblet of water. The woman made loud bubbling noises that made the children watching laugh even more, but made Kal's stomach lurch and his sight turned to the blackness of the big room.

"Hark, ye children, venerate the Venatores, for they stand as the chosen champions of the Gods. They shield us from the malevolence of Demons, monstrous fiends, Magic, and those who consort with its ilk." Kal hadn't realized that he had vomited until he finally noticed Freya patting his shoulder. People around Kal were looking at him with disgust. He was drawing too much attention. He needed to leave. No, he needed to run. The masks they were all wearing were wretched, soulless, horrific. They caused him to remember what he wanted to forget forever. Somehow, in his haste to hide, Kal found himself hyperventilating in one of the hundreds of unlit alleys… And he wasn't alone.

A half-starved man quietly approached them from behind. His hair was hidden under a hood, and his face was concealed behind a mask of a Saint too cracked to be recognizable. The half-starved man let his knife gently scrape around Kal's back, whispering, "Empty your pockets, or I will drown your little sister in your own blood!"

Kal turned, and his heart thundered. He was at risk, but more concerning to Kal, Freya was in danger. Kal attempted to formulate configurations to the Rules of Reality, but the intrusive memories wouldn't cease. The searing agony of icy knives carving his flesh for a decade on the Masked Ones' vivisection table. The shame and guilt for failing his only family and leaving her to rot in their Gods forsaken prison. Kal gagged as air refused to enter his lungs, and his hands quaked uncontrollably. The mugger had no knowledge of the horror going through Kal's head and saw that as a threat. The knife nearly plunged Kal's stomach but stopped and floated in mid-air. There was a soft blue glow behind Kal. He turned to see Freya reaching out her arms.

"You are… like me?" Kal asked, his voice quivering as his memories finally retreated to where they belonged and cleared his mind.

"DRAO-" The mugger tried to scream before Kal's sudden clarity allowed him to use Magic. He altered the Rules of Reality so gravity would force the mugger to fall sideways, reaching terminal velocity and crunching into the brick wall. The mugger's neck popped. Only Freya's crying could be heard in the sudden silence.

Kal sprinted out of the alleys before someone found what was left of the body. Freya was screaming, and he knew why. A few Magic Users in the Crusade mentioned that gaining Magical awareness was overwhelming as you suddenly sense every aspect of existence governed by the Rules of Reality and have not yet learned to tune it out. She would be experiencing intrusive and ceaseless formulations for every person held to the earth, for every light that enters her eyes, for every sound that enters her ears, for every rise and fall of heat around her, for everything. Most of the Magic Users were either in their teens or right before. Life-threatening circumstances can force the body to become aware sooner.

Freya was so very young. It must have been complete sensory overload. Kal realised his panic was only making things worse for Freya. He slowed his pace as soon as they were outside of town. Kal held her tightly to his chest and sat down in the snow.

Kal whispered, "Hush vennen lille min. Keep your eyes closed and listen to my heart." Freya's sob ridden breathing steadied with his own. He would have much to explain and little ways to describe it to such a young child. For now, they needed to catch their breath.

***

When they finally returned home, Kal let Freya stand on the wooden floor. She wobbled over to their cot and grabbed his potion recipe book. He had read out loud to her every night to help her sleep, but right now, he needed to tell her, to explain to her, "You are a Draoi."

"I don't wanna be a Draoi! I wanna be me!" Freya whined. Her face reddened as tears poured out of her eyes once more.

Kal was at least experienced enough with this to know where she was going. He spoke calmly, "It is all right, vennen lille min. You are not alone. I am one too."

Freya still sniffled but was able to quiet down after some time and some repeating.

"I did not tell you before because I did not know if you would be like me and you are so young, but now that we know… I promise to tell you everything from now on, and I need you to do the same. Can you promise me this, vennen lille min?"

She nodded and tried to hand the book to him again.

"Very well, vennen lille min. I will read until our eyes grow heavy."

WHAT'S COMING NEXT

Thank you again for reading this book and supporting me. As of the release of this book I am currently in the middle of writing the direct sequel to A Star of Ash: A Child of Magic that is called A Star of Ash: A Child from Faith. I'll be posting updates on my progress across various media outlets as well as additional lore of the world. If you wish to further help and support, please spread the word. The more people that check this out, the more time I can spend on it.

ABOUT THE AUTHOR

Follow me on Facebook, Twitter, or Tik Tok to learn more and ask me anything. Please don't spoil the book though.

https://www.facebook.com/profile.php?id=100090512516536

https://twitter.com/PDJs_Creations

https://www.tiktok.com/@parkers_creations?is_from_we bapp=1&se nder_device=pc